"You know what's sexy?"

Cal dragged one finger across Maggie's lips. It was the single sexiest move she'd ever experienced. "These lips."

Maggie swallowed hard. "Uh…"

"No, don't say it," he said, running his finger lightly back across her bottom lip. "I know you think it's a bad idea to mix business and pleasure, Maggie. Thing is, I don't really care."

He slid his hand across her jaw and cupped the back of her head, his fingers tangling in the hair pulled tight in her ponytail. Tilting her head back, he studied her face.

And she studied his. Long dark eyelashes totally wasted on a man framed eyes the color of a Caribbean surf. Lean jaw, firm chin and those damn lips she wanted to feel on her body…everywhere.

"I don't need this job, Maggie."

She inhaled deeply. "So why did you take it?"

"For this," he said, and lowered his head, his lips covering hers…

Dear Reader,

My first published book was set in Texas, and I'm happy to return to the Lone Star state in *Cowboy Crush*. There's something about a cowboy, right? That lazy walk, wide smile and worn blue jeans make a girl's heart gallop. Bull rider Cal Lincoln is definitely dangerous to the heart—he's naughty and bored, which means he's primed for the pretty city slicker who inherits a run-down ranch in the middle of nowhere.

Poor Maggie Stanton. The Triple J is supposed to be a piece of heaven on earth, but the gaping windows, leaking roof and feral cat problem say otherwise. She can sell the property, but first she'll have to do some repairs...and luckily the sexy cowboy recovering from surgery is available to lend a hand. Working hard is only tolerable when a gal can play hard, and Cal's also more than willing to be Maggie's playground. But what happens when fun turns into something more lasting? And a ranch turns into a home?

Good things—I know because I wrote the ending!

So I would love to hear what you think about Maggie and Cal. You can find me at liztalleybooks.com or come like my page on Facebook at liztalleybooks.

Happy reading,

Liz

Liz Talley

Cowboy Crush

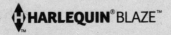

HARLEQUIN® BLAZE™

Recycling programs
for this product may
not exist in your area.

ISBN-13: 978-0-373-79885-8

Cowboy Crush

Copyright © 2016 by Amy R. Talley

This edition published by arrangement with Harlequin Books S.A.

For questions and comments about the quality of this book, please contact us at CustomerService@Harlequin.com.

Printed in U.S.A.

After being a finalist for RWA's prestigious Golden Heart Award in Regency romance, **Liz Talley** found a home writing sassy contemporary romance. Her first book, *Vegas Two Step*, starred a spinster librarian and debuted in June 2010. Since that time, Liz has published fourteen more Harlequin Superromance novels. Her stories are set in the South, where the tea is sweet, the summers are hot and the men are hotter. Liz lives in north Louisiana with her childhood sweetheart, two handsome children, three dogs and a mean kitty. You can visit Liz at liztalleybooks.com to learn more about her upcoming books.

Books by Liz Talley

Harlequin Blaze

A Wrong Bed Christmas
"Where There's Smoke"

Harlequin Superromance

Home in Magnolia Bend

The Sweetest September
Sweet Talking Man
Sweet Southern Nights

The Boys of Bayou Bridge

Waters Run Deep
Under the Autumn Sky
The Road to Bayou Bridge

To get the inside scoop on Harlequin Blaze and its talented writers, be sure to check out BlazeAuthors.com.

All backlist available in ebook format.

Visit the Author Profile page at Harlequin.com for more titles.

For my Starbucks stars—Winnie, Connie, Christopher and sometimes Dustin. And my plotting (not plodding) walkers Phylis and Jennifer. Being a writer is not so lonely when I have all of you beside me.

1

CAL LINCOLN WAS damned tired of the four walls in the fancy travel trailer he'd lived out of all over the country for the past few years. What had always been his haven away from the grit, the chicks and the testosterone of rodeo felt more like itchy wool pajamas now. Which is why he'd carried his sad ass down to the Barbwire Grill for a stack of Freda Gonzales's fluffy buttermilk hotcakes. He liked his cakes swimming in syrup and melted butter with a cup of coffee that could peel paint off the walls. The fact Willie Amos and his brother Jeb were raising hell at the cash register over a charge for extra bacon didn't bother him at all. In fact, it was the most excitement he'd had in weeks.

Until she walked in.

The door opened, spilling in light, and there she stood, brown hair falling in waves around bared shoulders. Two-inch straps held up a halter top thing that hugged a pair of magnificent breasts...or a really good padded bra. But it was her lips that got him. They were coated in glossy lipstick that was a soft pink. Made a man think of dirty, dirty things.

"Uh, hello," she said. Because everyone in the joint had stopped chewing, cussing and staring at their phones in order to feast their eyes on the cool drink of water framed in the doorway. Cal swore he could have heard a mouse fart.

"I'm looking for, uh, a Mr.—" she pulled a piece of paper out of a purse he happened to know cost the price of a lawn mower and squinted at the page "—Lowery. Anyone know Charlie Lowery?"

Freda glanced cautiously over to Cal. Then she lifted one shoulder. "Sure, I know him, but there ain't one good reason anyone would want to find him."

Cal took a sip of coffee, nodding at the truth. He no longer owed any loyalty to Charlie. If the man was in trouble, nothing Cal could do. That ship had sailed long ago.

The pretty lady allowed the swinging glass door with the words Barbwire Grill scrawled in—you guessed it—barbed wire to close behind her. The door bumped what looked to be a spectacular ass, pushing her forward. And that's when Cal got a look at pretty legs nicely highlighted by a pair of shoes that had a wedge. She looked sexy as hell, though he guessed she'd been going for sophisticated casual with the shorts and top. She gave a confident smile. "I'm assuming by your tone Mr. Lowery's a ne'er-do-well type?"

Freda glanced again at Cal. He didn't move a muscle.

"I reckon that's a good way to describe him," Freda said.

Cal noted the Amos brothers' eyes took on a particular gleam.

"Why you wantin' ol' Charlie for anyhow? Most people avoid him like they do cow shit. He ain't exactly friendly," Willie said, revealing his badly worn-down canines.

For the first time she looked wary. "I have an appointment with him."

Her accent was definitely not Southern. And sure as hell wasn't Texan. She sounded like some of those fillies who liked to frequent the rodeo arenas when they were vacationing in Vegas. Flashy jeans, too-white teeth and an upper-crust clipped tone. Of course, no matter the brand name on their jeans, they liked riding a cowboy just as well as the small-town Tammy Jos and Jolenes.

"An appointment?" Freda prodded, handing Willie his change with a no-nonsense glare. "For what?"

"Well, that's really not the point," the woman said, looking around the diner, which had thinned out once the sun had risen above the scraggly tree line. Coyote Creek wasn't known for lushness. Her gaze glanced off him, but he saw the telltale flicker acknowledging his presence.

He knew he was a good-looking son of a gun. He'd known it ever since he'd caught his mama's friends sneaking a peek when he came in from baseball practice. It was like being born rich. He used what he had to get ahead. He'd never had much but a good smile and tight ass. A kid, raised in a used single-wide trailer his daddy bought right before he ditched him and his mama, had to use what the Good Lord gave him to get by. So the dimples, the body made for sin and the aw-shucks charm were bread and butter for him.

But this woman didn't flutter over him. She had too much poise for that.

And despite her obvious frustration with Charlie not being where he was supposed to be, she gave off a cool air, like she couldn't be bothered with anyone in the dumpy two-horse town.

"What's the point, then?" Cal asked, finally piping up. Least he could do since Charlie was a no-good drunk who stuck to things like spit sliding off a greased pig.

The woman settled her gaze back on him. "I'm sorry. Perhaps, I wasn't clear. I'm trying to find the gentleman who was supposed to meet me at the town hall. I've been waiting since seven thirty this morning. I thought one of you might be willing to help me. Always heard Texans are friendly."

A challenge.

Cal dropped his feet from where they'd been propped on the opposite booth. His old boots made a decisive slap. He ignored the twinge of pain in his ribs. "You heard right. We're friendly. But when strangers amble in asking about one of ours, we sorta get suspicious-like."

He wanted to laugh at himself for the affected good-ol'-boy verbiage, but he couldn't help himself. Not only did she make him want to find out how good those slick lips tasted, but her horrified expression over the not-so-fancy diner and its salt of the earth patrons got his dander up. So they were hicks? Big deal. She didn't have to look like she'd stumbled on a den of cockroaches.

Okay, so maybe that was his presumption. She hadn't sniffed disdainfully or reached for hand sanitizer…yet.

She narrowed her eyes at him but then offered a nice smile. "I forgot my manners. Sorry. My name is Maggie Stanton. I'm here about the Triple J ranch. Technically, I'm the new owner."

Freda dropped a plate of sausage on the floor.

Willie elbowed Jeb, then doubled over, honking like a goose.

Punch, Freda's husband, turned from the setting of eggs he'd been scrambling on the grill and said, "Do what now?"

Cal wanted to join in the incredulous laughter, but the look on Maggie's face prevented him. She had no clue what she'd said.

"What's wrong?" she asked, looking confused. "Why is he laughing?"

Her gaze landed on Jeb, who looked as if he might collapse to the floor in a fit, so Cal stood and popped him a good one on the back.

"Ow," he squealed, straightening and rubbing his shoulder.

Cal pushed on by Big Willie and Jeb and walked to Maggie, who clutched her leather bag so tightly her knuckles turned white. First hint of being unnerved.

"I'm Cal," he said, sticking out the hand he could use fairly well. The dull throb in his opposite shoulder reminded him he still needed to pop the halved pain pill he carried in his front pocket.

She eyed his hand before setting her own in his. "Nice to meet you."

Of course he knew it wasn't really nice to meet him because she stood in a diner full of strangers who were laughing at her...or rather the idea she was the new owner of the dilapidated house and barn sitting on close to four hundred acres of hardscrabble.

"Why don't you let me buy you a cup of coffee?" he asked, shelving the hick routine. She didn't need that on top of the others' reactions.

Her brow furrowed. "But I really need to—"

"Just sit a spell. Punch makes the best coffee this side of the Brazos."

Punch lifted his flipper in salute and turned back to his grill. Freda watched with hawk eyes as Cal took Maggie's elbow and escorted her over to the booth he'd vacated seconds ago. Willie and Jeb recovered enough to waddle toward the exit. The two truck drivers both turned back to their steak-and-egg platters. Show over.

Maggie sat down, placing her bag on the bench beside her and her sunglasses on the table. "I don't understand what's going on."

He motioned for Freda. "You want coffee?"

"I don't drink coffee. Maybe some herbal tea?" she asked.

The face he made was answer enough.

"I'll have a diet soda," she said when Freda butted her rounded hips up to the table.

"Sure, we got that," Freda said, eyeing Cal. She tapped on her order pad for a few seconds. "And you watch out for this one here. He's got sweet words that'll have you outta your drawers before you can blink."

Maggie looked at Cal like he was a cottonmouth curled up on a rock.

Cal gave Freda his patented smile. "Don't be scaring the little lady just because Punch won't let you come play with me, *querida*."

"If I did play with you, cowboy, you'd have no good reason for looking for any other fun. I have a big playground right here," she said, smacking her large backside and laughing.

"Wait a sec, I'm here on business, not—" Maggie started.

"Relax, she's just flirting with me. Did you see Willie and Jeb? Ain't much to mess with around Coyote Creek."

Maggie gave a lift of a delicious shoulder. "Okay, so

can you give me some information about the Triple J, Mr.…"

"Lincoln. Cal Lincoln."

"As you can tell, I'm not from here."

"No way," he joked with a smile.

He saw her relax a little. "I'm from the Northeast actually. Uh, Philadelphia. This is my first time in Texas."

"Welcome to the Lone Star State."

"Thank you," she said with pretty manners. Her eyes were the color of smoky brown topaz. His mama had had a ring with the stone when he was a boy. She dragged it out every time she went to church…which wasn't much since she'd worked days at the Coyote Creek Motel. She'd loved that damn ring.

For a few seconds they didn't speak. Freda plopped a huge glass of Diet Coke down in front of Maggie. After a few seconds of neither Maggie nor Cal talking, Freda sighed and went back to her usual spot wiping the counter down. Her ear remained tuned in their direction.

"Are you kin to Old Man Edelman? He croak or something?"

"He passed away last month," Maggie said, her eyes shadowed with sadness. "He was a good man."

"You related to him?"

"No. I was his administrative assistant."

"How'd you end up with his place, then?"

Her expression grew guarded. "People down here sure are nosy."

"Part of being a Texan. We're friendly and nosy." Cal picked up his half-finished coffee and took a sip. It had grown cold so he motioned for Freda to give him a warm-up. She ignored him. "Might as well spill right here and now."

"Well, if you must know, he grew sick in his later years. I was his assistant, helping him run his day-to-day affairs. When he passed and the will was read, I found out he left the Triple J to me. I expected nothing, of course, since I was an employee. But Mr. Edelman was a good man. His children made a bit of a fuss, but what Bud Edelman wanted he got even in death."

Everyone in Coyote Creek knew old Bud Edelman had more money than hell had sin. He owned a company that sold ice cream all over the country. The Triple J had been a self-indulgent lark for the old tycoon. He'd shown up every summer for a month and played at being a cowboy before he went back to Pennsylvania and his millions. But the place hadn't been occupied in over ten years and had been left in the care of Charlie Lowery, an irresponsible drunk.

"That's quite a story," Cal said, eyeing this woman who'd flown out to look over the ranch. What in the world had possessed her to come to Coyote Creek? Nothing glamorous about the small Texas town, nothing particularly pretty about it, either. "But why did you come all the way out here?"

She looked at him like he was a moron. Which some would say was accurate but Cal wasn't admitting to it. "Because I'm a responsible person who can't ignore something she's been gifted. I called the town hall to inquire about the property and someone named Millie gave me Mr. Lowery's name and number. Took me a week to get in touch with him. He told me the place needed a good scrubbing, but there were cows and a horse. He wanted me to wire him money. But I'd rather meet him and view the property in person."

"If you were Bud's assistant, how come you didn't know all that to begin with?"

She looked annoyed at the question. "Mr. Edelman liked to take care of matters with the Triple J himself. My job was to transfer money into the ranch account. He handled everything else."

"Millie should have given you the number to a good realty company and saved you the trip out here."

"You're assuming I'm selling the place?" she asked, placing those plump lips around the straw. He noticed. Gosh damn, did he notice those lips.

"I ain't assuming nothing. Tell you what. I'll drive you out to the ranch," he said. She needed to see what she was getting herself into. He hadn't been out that way since he'd come home last time, but he knew all the local kids sneaked out there to drink and shoot Coke cans. Someone had mentioned a load of feral cats in the barn, too. Supposedly, Charlie had allowed it to slide into disrepair which was a damn shame because it had once been a nice place.

"I need the keys. Otherwise I could have gone myself, Mr. Lincoln. I do have a navigation system."

Cal smiled. "Of course you do, but the thing is, some of these Texas roads aren't on the map."

"This one is. But I figured it would have a gate or something. Mr. Lowery said he'd bring all the keys and show me around. I'm not sure I could even get on the property without a key."

Cal smiled. "I guarantee I'll get you to the front door."

"I suppose I can follow you in my rental," she said, like any good city girl who knew better than to climb into a pickup truck with a stranger wearing Wranglers with holes in the knees. Of course his straw hat was new and expensive...not that a girl from Philly would know.

"Sure," he said, motioning for the check. This time Freda hurried over.

"You paying for her Coke?" she asked, hooking an eyebrow.

"No, here, let me," Maggie said, reaching for her bag.

Cal plopped a twenty down on the handwritten ticket Freda had ripped off and sat on the chipped Formica. "I always buy pretty ladies a drink."

Maggie made a frowny face which made her look cute. Still sexy. But cute, too. "Thank you."

"Keep the change, Freda. I'm going to take Mrs.... Miss?"

"Miss," Maggie conceded.

"Miss Stanton out to the Triple J. Send the sheriff if I ain't back in two days," he joked as he grabbed his hat and slid out of the booth.

He was damned glad to know she wasn't married. Not that it really mattered. She'd take one look at that dump out on Highway 139 and all he'd see was a trail of dust out of Coyote Creek. In fact as soon as his body healed, he'd be hitting the road, too. The day-to-day boredom paired with his mother harping about him getting killed, about him finding something safer to do...about him being too much like his deadbeat father drove him crazy. His cracked ribs were better and the punctured lung had healed, but his shoulder still hurt like a bitch. His agent called every other day wanting to know his progress. PBR and PRCA reps called, too. His sponsors emailed him. Friends texted him. Everyone wanted him back on the tour come August, except for his mother. And maybe the bulls. They'd never liked him much 'cause he could stay on almost half the time.

"Wait," Maggie said, rising beside him. "Why would someone have to come get us? What are you guys not telling me about this place?"

"No worries, Maggie," he said, gesturing toward the door before sliding the pill out of his pocket and popping it in his mouth. Only half the dosage. He had to wean himself from the painkillers. "I'm banged up but perfectly capable of looking after you."

"I don't need looking after. I'm a grown woman," she said, quite serious about it.

"Don't think I didn't notice," he said, refusing to slide his eyes suggestively down her body like he wanted to. Didn't want her to think he was a pervert. She looked skittish enough at the thought of following him out to the Triple J.

Freda snapped her fingers. "See? Don't say I didn't warn you about this cowboy."

Maggie shouldered her bag and perched her sunglasses atop her head. Then she gave Freda a wry smile. "I'll be sure to keep my legs crossed."

Cal barked a laugh. "I want to see you drive with your legs crossed."

Maggie let a self-deprecating laugh escape. "Dear Lord, what am I doing?"

"I don't know," Cal said, pushing open the door to greet the sunny morning. "But I'm kinda glad you're doing it with me this morning. I've been bored as hell around here."

2

MAGGIE WIPED A sweaty palm against her linen shorts and focused on the hot cowboy's tailgate, which bumped down the dusty highway at a fast clip. Nothing like a man in worn jeans who drove fast and talked slow. She wondered what other things he did slowly.

Then she swallowed hard and warned her libido that now was not the time to get interested in a man.

Of course, there had been too much of telling herself no over the past several years, which is probably why she'd noticed just how sexy one Mr. Cal Lincoln was. Being the personal and administrative assistant to Herbert "Bud" Edelman, owner of Edelman Enterprises, was a big job, but it was one she did surprisingly well. Growing up the fatherless child of the Edelman estate's housekeeper had given Maggie a set of valuable skills— she was diplomatic, humble and hardworking. After college, she had planned on taking a position with a law firm, with the idea of applying for law school in the back of her mind, but life had a way of putting a person down where it wanted. Bud had needed her, so she'd taken advantage of the salary and security…and found out she was a damn good administrator. Her competency had allowed an ailing Bud to untie himself from his work and focus on recovering from his debilitating stroke.

But now her mentor was gone.

She glanced over at the box containing Bud's ashes resting on her floorboard and tried not to tear up.

No time for tears, turkey.

The pickup in front of her slowed. To her left she saw a rusted sign arcing above the entrance to the ranch. From either side, fencing stretched across as far as she could see. Tall grass waved in the ditches and the land rose up so she couldn't see where the graveled road led. Three rusty *J*s were woven into the sign. The Triple J had been named after Bud's three children—James, Julien and Judith. All worthless idiots too busy to visit their father unless they needed money. Which meant they'd come by the estate fairly regularly.

Cal pulled in and put his truck into Park. She pulled in beside him, eyeing the locked gate, and rolled down the window of the rental car.

He climbed out, leaving his pickup running. "Let me look at the lock."

He moseyed toward the padlock holding a length of chain threaded through the gates. He studied it and then let it drop, clanking against the metal. Then he moseyed back to his truck, opened the lid of a trunk thing in the back and brought out a large pair of bolt cutters. One hard squeeze—which caused a flash of pain across Cal's face—and the chain fell uselessly to the side.

Turning, he gave her a dimpled grin that made heat shoot into her belly. "Don't need keys in Texas."

"So I see," she said, glancing back at the lock before returning her gaze to the cowboy. Cal wasn't a big man, but he covered a lot of ground with his broad shoulders and tight ass. He looked like a rodeo queen's dream with his ambling walk, lazy grin and naughty blue eyes beneath the brim of the cowboy hat.

Cal kicked the two gates open and then gestured. "Ladies first."

She pulled past the gate and waited for him to climb back into his truck. He shifted into Drive and followed her over the hill and down the path.

Her first impression was that Bud had been right. The Triple J was a piece of heaven on earth with wide, waving pastures, dotted with occasional scrubby brush. Shady trees she couldn't identify framed a rippling pond, and a picturesque red barn sprawled not far away from several paddocks and a low building that looked like a hall of some sort. Situated to the right was a white farmhouse with a huge porch that sagged, broken windows that yawned and a roof covered by blue tarp signifying a leak. A skin-and-bones nag looked lonely in the far pasture, and when Maggie rolled up next to the house, about eight cats scattered from the yard, reminding her of a drug bust she'd once seen in a bad part of Philly.

Her heart sank.

"Shit," she whispered as the tiny worm of an idea that she might have been gifted a new future shriveled up.

"Well, this is it," Cal said, hopping down from his cab and slamming the truck door.

Maggie climbed out, shielding her eyes. "This is not what I expected."

He surveyed the run-down ranch house. "Never is, is it?"

Truer words were never spoken.

"What's with all the cats?" she asked.

"Dunno, feral cat problem?"

"Feral cat," she repeated, walking over to the lonely horse.

"On the bright side, you probably don't have much of a rat problem," he said.

"Mmm," she said, looking over the horse that looked as if it hadn't been fed in weeks. She lifted a hand to its nose, though she'd only ever touched the nose of a pony at a friend's birthday when she was eight years old. The horse blew out a gentle breath. "Is this horse malnourished?"

Cal walked to the beast. The horse turned toward him as if it knew he could be trusted. It blew again as he stroked the coat with his strong hands. "Hey, now, old gal, hey."

His words soothed even her.

"Nah, she's just old. Ain't ya, girl?" Cal slapped a hand against the horse's neck. "Let's check the barn."

She turned to the red barn and noted the graffiti scrawled across it. Some very naughty words along with the rendering of a giant penis graced the front. "Nice artwork."

"Yeah, the kids in town come out here to drink and screw. This old place has probably seen more action than a Reno whorehouse."

The barn doors had been busted open, so Cal didn't have to fetch the bolt cutters again. Empty dusty stalls and an old tractor met them. Bags of feed spilled over. Several cats peeked out and she heard mewling kittens somewhere in the dank hay. "This is a mess. What in the hell has this Lowery guy been doing with the money I moved into the ranch accounts each month?"

Cal shrugged. "The animals are alive."

"You sure? I didn't see the thirty head of cattle that supposedly roam the ranch."

"Probably in the back field. Shade trees there and it'll be plenty hot today," Cal said, wiping a hand over his brow. The back of his T-shirt already showed dampness.

Maggie didn't want to show her disappointment in front of the cowboy...if he even was a cowboy. Just because a man wore boots, a hat and Wranglers didn't mean he was a cowboy. In her limited experience thus far, lots of Texans wore cowboy stuff no matter what their profession. "What am I supposed to do with this?"

"Sell it. It needs work, but you can get something out of it. I don't know much about the real estate market, but it's good acreage."

Of course, selling the ranch was the smartest option. Wasn't like she was actually interested in owning a ranch, but the terms of the will made it complicated. If she kept the ranch for five years, the title would be hers. If she sold it, the profit would be split with the Edelman children, with her only getting a fourth of the sale. Maggie's first thought was to hold on to the property for the required years, but she didn't have the money needed to both maintain a ranch and support herself in Philadelphia. If it hadn't been so dilapidated, the money netted from the sale would be plenty to help her start a new life, but as is...

She sucked in a deep breath. "How do I find Mr. Lowery?"

"Try the bars."

"Which one?"

"All of 'em."

Great. Bud had been paying a drunk to take care of the place. The old man's pride and joy, the surprise bequest he'd left her, had been abandoned for a bottle of whiskey.

Piece of heaven her ass.

Maggie pinched the bridge of her nose. "I can sell, but I'll have to fix it first. No one's going to make an offer on something needing this much work."

"Sure they will. Sell it 'as is.'"

She leveled a look at Cal. "Would you buy this place?"

"Shit, no."

"Exactly. That will be everyone's response. And since I need the money this place will bring, I want top dollar. How much do you think this place would be worth with over three hundred and fifty acres and a decent—" she tossed a glance at the pathetic house "—house?"

Cal looked at the house, squinting his eyes. "Well, it's a big house. If you repaired it, painted it, upgraded some things inside, you'd probably get a couple of million easy. Land's prized around here, but a working ranch, spiffed up…"

"So you don't know?"

"Not really. Like I said, real estate's not my thing."

Which made her wonder—what was his thing?

But what did Cal matter at that moment? She had bigger fish to fry. Her original plan when she'd left Philly had been to stay a day or two, scatter Bud's ashes and make the decision on what to do with the Triple J. Of course, she knew the right decision would be to sell the place. But Bud had talked about the Triple J with such wistfulness, describing nights in front of the fireplace, rocking chairs on the porch and lovely vistas. In the back of her mind, Maggie had wondered if the ranch could be a place to belong even if she didn't know a gelding from a stallion. She could finally have something that was all hers, silly as it sounded.

The Triple J would be sold. Maggie would take her part and head back to the East Coast. She could stay with her aunt until she found her own place. And though she'd sent her résumé to several companies and already netted interview requests, she'd been kicking around the idea of starting her own consulting firm. She was particularly skilled in creating and facilitating successful board meetings. If she could parlay that skill into a company that mediated contentious corporate situations, she could be her own boss. But to do that, she needed seed money.

"I need to think. Renovating this place will be a huge job," she said, trying to regain some of the cool she'd lost in the past few minutes. The situation called for being rational, strategic and—

"I could help you out," Cal said, interrupting her internal plea for calmness.

"What?"

"Right now I'm living in a trailer on my mom's land… at least for the next month, but I could always move out here and oversee repairs."

"Are you a…uh, carpenter? Or contractor?"

His smile was like sun after a storm. "Hell, no."

"I'm not sure why I would hire someone who doesn't have any skills to oversee something that… Well, I'm not even sure of the extent of what's needed." So he was unemployed, lived in a trailer on his mother's land and looking for a job? Sounded like a man to stay away from.

"I have skills," he said, an edge in his words implying he was talking about more than using a hammer.

Maggie clamped her mouth closed and studied him. In the midmorning light, he looked right as rain framed against the faded barn. He had the whole fantasy thing going—sexy cowboy with a side of trouble.

Or a side of fun.

Okay, yeah, she was attracted to him. Very attracted to him. He made little butterflies flit around her tummy and warmth curl up her spine. But that wasn't a good enough reason to employ someone she'd not even vetted to help her out of a tight spot with the Triple J.

Just as she was about to open her mouth to turn down his offer, generous or not, a pickup truck bumped over the rise. The paint job was interesting—two doors covered in white primer and a hood painted bright blue. The rest of the vehicle was a rusty red. It looked like a worn-out American flag as it came to a halt beside Cal's truck. The engine died and an older man climbed out.

Cal rubbed a hand over his face. "Ah, shit."

"You the gal I'm supposed to meet?" the older man called in a gravelly voice, walking toward them. He wore a straw cowboy hat, brand-new indigo jeans and a T-shirt with Rattled Rooster Saloon stamped across the front. He spit in the dust and eyed Cal.

The tension between the men was thick. Like there could be a shoot-out at the not-so-OK Corral.

"The gal?" Maggie repeated, not bothering to extend her hand.

The older man lifted his hat. "Sorry about being late. Set my damn alarm clock for p.m. and not a.m. I'm usually up when the cock crows, but I must have been tuckered out."

Cal snorted.

Charlie's mouth tightened at the sound.

"I'm assuming you're Mr. Lowery?"

The man nodded.

"I accept your apology. But what I do not accept is the condition of this ranch. You've been paid a considerable sum of money each month to take care of the Triple J and you've failed miserably."

Charlie drew back. "Now see here, Ms....what's your name again?"

"Stanton."

"What you don't understand is how much money it takes to run a ranch. It's more than feed and vet bills. I asked Bud for extra money to fix the barn and repaint it last year. Those damn kids are always out here drinking and fu—uh, messing around. Only so much I can do. I told him about the roof leaking. He said he'd send somebody. So I tried."

"Tried?" Maggie reined in the anger brewing inside her. "I'll need to see your accounting, Mr. Lowery."

"Like receipts and stuff? Might be a few on the floorboard, but Bud never told me I had to keep a book or nothing."

"You realize you're going to make restitution, don't you? This place is in shambles."

Charlie looked over at Cal who stood still as a puddle watching the confrontation. "What are you doing here?"

Before Cal could say anything, Maggie pointed a finger toward Charlie. "He's the person who is going to oversee you and the cleanup of the Triple J. Consider Cal the foreman on this project. And you're going to be intimately involved with rectifying the neglect or I'll sue your pants off."

She hadn't meant to make Cal the foreman...which wasn't actually a position for something like this. Or maybe it was. She'd never undertaken the salvaging of a ranch. Lawyering up was merely a threat. Though she was certain she could get the attorney Bud had used for forty years to draft a threatening letter. Regardless she had to get the place cleaned up and Charlie Lowery owed her. Lumping Cal in was sheer insanity. Maybe the horniness she had for the man had blocked out logic. Or perhaps it was the image of him lifting boards and painting fences, shirtless and glistening with sweat in the hot Texas sun.

Oh, God. She needed to have her head examined. Or get laid.

Or both.

Charlie's face registered agitation. "You're hiring Cal? He's not a contractor. He's a bu—"

"I'm perfectly capable of overseeing the repairs," Cal interrupted. "If you remember, I spent many summers working ranches."

Charlie didn't say anything more in argument. He merely shifted his gaze from Cal to her and then back to Cal again. After a few tense seconds, he uttered, "This is bullshit."

And then he stalked to his truck, lowered the tailgate and hefted a heavy bag to his shoulder. Without another word to either of them, he disappeared into the barn. Five or six cats followed him, their heads ducked cautiously.

Cal turned back to her. "You're really going to hire me?"

"I wasn't planning on it."

"But…"

She sucked in more hot Texas air. "Honestly, you're the only person I know here. And you were true to your word—you got me inside the ranch. And I don't have time to do a huge job search. Please tell me you have some actual experience with—" she threw her hands in the air and spun around surveying the Triple J "—working miracles?"

"They call me the miracle worker," he said.

She arched her brow.

"Okay, they don't, but I spent every summer in high school working ranches and construction. If I can't do it, I'll find someone who can."

Maggie squeezed her eyes closed and tried to center herself. This was going to be a huge undertaking and would cost a pretty penny. She had forty thousand dollars in savings and maybe five thousand in her checking account. No way would she cash out any investments. But if she wanted to sell the Triple J for more than a marginal profit, she'd have to spend some cash. Starting with Cal. "How much?"

"For what?"

"To get this place ready to list? I'm assuming you're unemployed otherwise you wouldn't have offered your services." Her tongue nearly tripped on those last words. They'd sounded suggestive, though she'd not intended them to be.

A strange expression crossed his face, but he caught himself. "Four thousand. Should take about five or six weeks if the rain stays away. It's mid-July so I don't see an issue there. Probably have to hire some pros for some stuff, but I know a few guys who are good and won't charge an arm and a leg."

"That seems fair. I'll draw up a contract."

"But I need to inspect the place first. Let's meet at the Barbwire tomorrow morning," Cal said before jerking his head toward the barn. "A word of warning—Charlie has a drinking problem and a habit of interfering where he's not wanted."

"He owes Bud recompense. The shape this place is in rests on his shoulders. Find something for him to do, or I'll sue him for breach of contract." Maggie wasn't sure if the contract would hold up since most of the terms were unwritten. But she'd bluff her way through. Charlie was a free laborer and *free* sounded good at the moment.

Cal shrugged. "Your rodeo."

Yeah. A big, fat, disastrous one where she stood in the center of the arena wearing a barrel as her underwear like those funny rodeo clowns she'd seen in cartoons. "I'm heading back to town. I have a lot to do in order to relocate to Coyote Creek."

"Relocate? You're not going back to Pennsylvania?" Cal asked.

"After ten years of paying someone to do a job that didn't get done, you think I'm going to leave this place unattended? If I'm plopping down money, I'm part of the process."

"Define 'part of the process.'"

"I'm a hard worker. I'll pitch in."

Cal lowered his gaze, taking in the new wedge sandals she'd scored on a half-price rack last week and the secondhand Louis Vuitton bag her cousin had bought at a yard sale. She could see his thoughts in those pretty blue eyes. He thought she was useless. "You're going to help clean and repair the Triple J?"

"I know how to hold a paintbrush," she said, sliding her sunglasses back in place. "As soon as I contact animal control about these cats, I'll get the house habitable."

Cal might have smirked, but she didn't wait around to see. Cowboy Cal and Grumpy Charlie may have preconceived notions about her, but they didn't know her veneer of sophistication had been shellacked on to survive the snooty world of the Edelmans. Her mother had been the housekeeper and Maggie had scrubbed many a toilet and polished many a silver serving tray. Hard Work was her middle name.

"You're going to stay in the house?" Cal called to her.

Maggie glanced over at the sad dwelling. Poor place looked as if it had cashed in on existing. But at one time, the Triple J ranch house had been a home. "Have you seen the Coyote Creek motel?"

Cal twisted lips that made her think of morning sex. "Good point."

Maggie climbed into the car, watching the cowboy through her windshield. He surveyed the house and then walked around back, perhaps looking for a place to park his trailer.

So many questions about him rambled around her mind, but she supposed there would be time for answers. After all, they'd be working together for the next month or so. The faster she sold the Triple J, the faster she could get on with her life.

Maggie slid an apologetic glance to the box holding the ashes of her late boss.

"Sorry, Bud. I know you hoped I'd fall in love with the Triple J, but I don't even own cowboy boots."

Though she might want to grab a pair if she was going to be here for a while.

3

THREE DAYS LATER Cal watched Maggie dip the sponge into the bucket of soapy water and scrub down the front door of the Triple J ranch house. Ten years of lightning bug and moth waste dotted the wooden door with the broken glass insets. Would have been easier to buy a whole new damn door, but Miss Maggie Stanton was tighter than Dick's hatband when it came to letting go of cash.

She looked damned fine in a pair of cutoff shorts that cupped her ass, a loose tank top and sandals that allowed toenails of bright red to peek out. Her brown ponytail bobbed as she uttered indiscriminant curse words under her breath. Stepping back she tossed the sponge into the bucket, splashing soapy water onto the sagging porch boards.

"Damn it."

He climbed the steps, avoiding the one with the loose board. "Looks better."

"No, it doesn't, but at least it's clean." She brushed her hands on her shorts. The waistband dipped giving

him a glimpse of apple-green panties. She turned to him.
"Did you call the guy about the leak?"

"Yeah. The roofing company's sending a guy for an
estimate."

"The roof has to be fixed before we can do any other
work inside. And there's a lot of work to be done."

Cal looked at the door and then pulled a small notebook from his back pocket. He added "paint front door"
to the list. "I'm heading to physical therapy, but I'll be
back by five o'clock. The painters will be out in the barn.
If you have a problem, call me."

"So I'm supervising now?" Her eyes dipped down to
his chest. He knew he'd sweated buckets and his T-shirt
clung to him. He'd been helping Ray and his team tear
out rotten boards and replace them on the west side of
the barn. Her noticing the clinging material made something naughty rear up inside him. One thing he knew
was when a woman was interested. He'd caught Maggie's
gaze on him more than once. Firm indicator.

Two mornings ago, he and Maggie had come to an
agreement regarding the renovation of the Triple J over
pancakes at the Barbwire Grill. He had no clue why
he'd agreed to help Maggie. Okay, he did. Some of it
was wanting to get away from living with his mom and
her husband. After the wreck on Rasputin, his mother
had resurrected her petition that he give up bull riding.
And some of it was feeling bad his old mentor had allowed the ranch to fall into disrepair. But most of it had
to do with the insane attraction he held for Maggie. It
had been months since he'd felt any interest in a woman.
Maybe longer than that. Occasionally when he won big
and drank enough, he took advantage of the willing

women who frequented the bars. Yet he never felt anything more than a passing attraction.

Until Maggie had walked in.

Of course, he *was* bored and depressed by the lack of healing in his shoulder. He'd spent the past two weeks in bed watching *Divorce Court* and champing at the bit to get back to competing for the million-dollar prize. So doing a little work would make the hours go faster and being able to eye the sexy Maggie Stanton while doing it would be an added bonus.

So he made the list and hired the crews to repair the outer buildings for a ranch he cared nothing about. After inspecting the buildings, he'd decided the barn was too big of a job to attempt alone. He'd asked around and found a crew of painters who'd had a job fall through. They'd started work that morning, prepping for repainting right after the county animal control had picked up ten full traps of angry, snarling cats. Cal had started working on repairing stalls, carefully using his bad shoulder, hoping the natural movement might do some good since the prescribed therapy hadn't done what he'd hoped. Still hurt like hell, but the therapist said moving it was good for him.

Charlie had shown up midmorning and with a grunt started helping. Cal didn't have much left for the old man…or at least that's what he told himself.

Charlie had taken him under his wing when Cal had been a restless green buck set on causing trouble rather than being useful. The former rodeo star had taught Cal how to be a cowboy, watching Cal ride his first bull, teaching him how to position his hands and when to use the spurs. Once upon a time, Cal had worshiped Charlie.

Until the curmudgeonly cowboy had started drinking too much…and hitting on Cal's mother.

When Cal was in high school, his lonely mom had shared a few meals with Charlie. She'd seen it as casual companionship, two people who cared about Cal spending time together. But when she met Gary Whitehorse, Charlie got jealous. It spilled over onto Cal's rodeo life. The dam broke when Charlie tried to play daddy, demanding Cal quit bull riding after a particularly dangerous ride. Cal and Charlie had clashed like only two hardheaded fools could and the result was a sixteen-year silence. But Cal supposed they could hand each other nails and measure two-by-fours without talking much.

"I told you I'd have to go to physical therapy twice a week," he reminded her.

Maggie silently regarded Cal. He knew her thoughts, namely the unstated question of why he went to a physical therapist. He hadn't revealed he was a bull rider yet and he didn't know why he withheld the information. All he'd accomplished was something to be proud of, but after years of buckle bunnies hopping after him and reporters haggling him, he was tired of the fascination. Being a regular dude felt good. Like pulling on an old pair of blue jeans.

"Right," she said when she realized he wasn't going to explain. "Oh, so you know, I checked out of the motel. I'm staying here tonight."

"But the windows are still busted."

"I found the screens in the attic. Cats are gone and I'm tired of motel life."

"But it's hotter than hell without AC." His thoughts flickered to an image of her in a short nightie, sweat glistening between her breasts. Maybe no air-conditioning would be a good thing, especially since he'd pulled his trailer out this morning and had a nice view of the house. Of course, he wasn't a pervert who'd sit around, peering out his blinds, trying to catch a peek. But if she did venture out to the saggy porch in her barely there nightie, he damned sure wasn't looking away.

"I'll manage. Just get those guys from the hardware place out here tomorrow to replace the panes. Oh, and call the roofing company again. No rain in the forecast, but if a storm blows up, I don't want to have to get pans out."

"I'll put in another call, boss."

"Are you staying here tonight?" she asked, looking down at the bucket and eyeing the door again.

"Are you asking me to keep you company tonight, darlin'? 'Cause I'm more than willing."

Maggie's head jerked up. "That's not what I meant and you know it. I was thinking about safety."

"You can't blame a guy for wanting to keep a pretty filly company."

"Are you comparing me to a horse?" she asked, her brown eyes flashing. He loved her feisty spirit…which explained the teasing. Ruffling her feathers could become an addiction.

"You say it like being a horse is a bad thing. I like horses."

She rolled her eyes. "Mr. Lincoln, our relationship is strictly a working one. I'm not in the market for being your…filly."

"But you'll settle for being my nag?" he cracked.

That made her lips twitch. "On second thought, I prefer filly. And hasn't anyone ever suggested to you and to half of Texas that calling women *baby*, *honey* and *filly* is offensive?"

"If I kiss you and whisper 'baby, you're driving me wild,' you'd be offended?"

Maggie swallowed. "Yes."

"I'll file that away for—"

"Not for future reference. We can't... I mean, you are..." Maggie clamped her mouth closed, a faint pink creeping into her cheeks. He'd only known her for three days, but already he knew flustering Miss Priss was more fun than staring at Charlie's sad ass all day long. Maggie pulled on her business face, but he sensed the flirting pleased her. Like she was a woman who needed a little teasing in her life.

"Relax, Mags," he said, giving her a wink. "I never graze in a pasture if the gate ain't open."

Then he walked away at a slow ramble, knowing it would aggravate her. He'd bet his boots she loved cocky in a man and that's something he held by the bucket load. He was short on a lot of things—manners, stature and patience at times—but knowing who he was and what cards he held had always been his best quality. Which was why this injury had thrown him for a loop. He'd done everything required of him to no avail. Everyone kept saying "give it time," but that was something he didn't have. He had to be back on a bull soon with an eye on the standings if he wanted a shot at the money and title.

When Rasputin had stepped on his shoulder, he'd shattered the bones along with cracking two ribs. Then he'd tossed Cal, puncturing a lung in the process. All ornery eighteen hundred pounds of snot, muscle and fury, Rasputin was up for Bull of the Year for good reason. And Cal knew he'd probably draw the bastard again in one of the last few events before Nationals. He finished the first half ranked number four, but the points were close this year. Come mid-August he had to be ready. But because the injury had been on his left side and his shoulder didn't have good mobility, his balance was still shit.

He'd see about putting a bucking barrel in one of the stalls in the barn. He needed to practice and wasn't ready to ride anything that breathed yet. Or maybe he was…just not a bull.

But until he could get back in the proverbial saddle, he'd head to therapy where he'd sweat buckets, cuss like a sailor and pray his shoulder's flexibility improved. August wasn't far away.

MAGGIE WIPED THE sweat from her forehead and surveyed her efforts. The screens were in place and she'd managed to give the kitchen, living area and one bedroom a decent scrubbing. She'd ordered a new mattress but until it arrived, she'd make do on one in a bedroom that had been closed off. She found sheets in a linen closet and ran them through the washing machine that, praise Jesus, still worked. Currently they flapped in the hot Texas breeze, pinned to the old-fashioned wash line she'd found and strung up on the two old poles behind the house.

She glanced out at the barn, relieved to see the painters had accomplished a good bit in one day. Thankfully, they'd primed over the rude graffiti so she didn't have to stare at the rendering of the giant penis.

Waving at the men who loaded into a van, she went

back into the oven, aka the house, to fix something for dinner. A knock on the door stopped her.

Charlie stood on the porch, wiping his face with a faded bandana. "I'm leaving now."

"Okay," she said.

"How many days I gotta put in to satisfy you?" He looked grumpy as an old bullfrog.

"As many as it takes to get this place back to where it was when Bud entrusted it to you."

Charlie wiped a hand over his face. "Goddamn it. That could be next year. I ain't got time for this. I got my own shit to do."

"Like supporting the local bars? Don't you feel remorse for letting this place fall apart?" She crossed her arms and gave him her best boardroom stare. Yeah, there were times she had to be Bud's junkyard dog…in heels, of course.

"I did what I was hired to do. You can't blame me."

"Then whom shall I blame?"

"I don't give a damn. Blame Bud. I told him I needed more money."

"There was plenty of money in the ranch accounts."

Charlie frowned. "You don't understand the cost of running a ranch, but you'll see. Everything's expensive. Wait till you get the first vet bill. Bud only gave me so much and I took care of the animals first. Then I maintained the fence lines. I left the house for last. Wasn't nobody here no how. Every time I replaced the glass in the windows, those damn kids broke them again. I painted over the graffiti twice. Started seeming like a waste if you asked me."

The older man had a point. "Why not get to the root of the problem? Call the sheriff and put up cameras."

Charlie's mouth tipped into a smirk and she could see he'd once been a handsome man. "Think I didn't? Sheriff can only do so much. This is Texas and there's a lot of land to cover for his deputies. They came by and ran off some kids every now and again. And so you know, I set out game cameras. The one video feed I got was so grainy I couldn't tell if it was kids smoking pot or aliens."

"So you gave up?" Maggie asked.

Charlie shrugged. "Them kids beat me. But I'll help you out even if I have to put up with Cal bustin' my balls. Guess I owe Bud that much." Charlie shuffled back off the porch.

At that moment, Cal's truck bumped down to the barn. Charlie didn't say anything else. Just hustled toward his American flag truck, passing Cal without a word. Made her wonder why the older man didn't like Cal. Cal didn't bother acknowledging Charlie, either.

As he climbed the porch steps, Cal doffed his hat. She pushed outside onto the porch and sat down on the steps she'd swept off earlier to mostly get rid of spiders. Cal eased himself down so he sat on the same step. He smelled like the heat that surrounded them and faintly like menthol. "Painters gone?"

"A few minutes ago," she said, easing away from him, telling herself it was because he needed more shoulder room but knowing it was because she didn't want to be any more tempted than she already was. She had a hang-up for a cowboy. Never in a million years would she have guessed boots and a cowboy hat were such crack.

"Looks like they got a good bit done. On the way to McKinney I called about the septic system, AC and the wells. We need to get those checked and repaired," he said, setting his hat back on his head. Guess he took it off when greeting a lady. They sure were strange in Texas. But she was glad for it because she liked his hair. The locks were thick and shaggy. Perfect for running a woman's hands through.

What was he talking about? Oh, yeah, wells and septic systems.

Everything was so overwhelming, and she had much to learn about a ranch and Texas and…snakes. She'd seen one of the native reptiles coiled in the middle of the road today. She needed a book to help her out. Like *How to Run a Ranch for Dummies*. Or maybe there was a YouTube video. Seemed to be one for everything. She'd learned how to fold sheets and fix a vacuum cleaner on there.

Her face must have portrayed her frustration because Cal patted her thigh. "Just one forkful at a time."

His hand on her bared skin made heat slither into her belly. Correction. It made more heat slither into her belly. She was already hot as hell from her day of cleaning. And none too attractive she had to add. Maggie hadn't sweated this much since she'd tried hot yoga. "What?"

"That's how they say you eat an elephant, right? One forkful at a time."

"Who eats an elephant, anyway?"

"Dunno."

"Why are you going to therapy?" she asked.

He rubbed his hands against the worn denim of his jeans and stared out at the sun hovering over the horizon. "Shattered some bones in my left shoulder. Had surgery mid-May to fix it."

"That sounds painful," she said, wanting to peer

around him to look at his shoulder as if she could see through the cotton fabric. "Was it a wreck?"

"Actually it was." He smiled. "But it wasn't in a car."

"Motorcycle?" He'd look fine straddling a hog. She could see him riding with mirrored sunglasses and a badass smile. No clue how he'd manage to keep the cowboy hat on, though.

"Nah. Bull."

"Bull? You ran into a bull?"

"More like it knocked me out cold and then stepped on me," he said.

"Were you working with it? Like on a ranch?" Maybe he'd been a ranch hand. Or a real cowboy who drove cattle. But where did they drive cattle these days? From field to field? She hadn't a clue. Another thing she needed to learn.

"Actually I was riding it," Cal said, clasping his hands together between his spread knees.

"As in a rodeo?" Maggie asked, turning toward him. "That's, like, superdangerous." And it explained why he lived in a trailer on his mother's land. She didn't know much about rodeo, but she knew the cowboys who went town to town in search of rides didn't have much money. She'd listened to Garth Brooks's songs when she was a kid. Rodeo was a hard life.

"Yeah, it's dangerous. I've been gored, tossed, stepped on, and I've had stitches. Look—" he pulled off his cowboy hat and showed her a white puckered scar near his hairline "—that came from Nitro II. Threw that big head back and nailed me good."

"So you ride the bulls?"

"I ride the bulls. Well, some of the time."

"Huh," she said, lifting herself from the step. "I guess

I shouldn't ask if you're any good after looking at those injuries. You want to join me for supper?"

He looked up, blue eyes amused. She hadn't a clue why. He was the one who admitted to doing a completely asinine thing like climbing onto the back of a huge beast with horns. "What you having?"

"Well, you can have a ham sandwich, a turkey sandwich or Kraft mac and cheese. The Stop-N-Go had very little to offer in way of variety, though I did consider the wieners on the wiener-go-round."

Cal stood. "Wiener-go-round?"

"You know, that little thingy that rotates the wieners," she said, holding open the door.

"Is this sexy talk?" he asked, his eyes moving down her body.

"You sure you didn't get kicked in the head? 'Cause I'm pretty sure overcooked hot dogs are not sexy. Never have been, never will be."

Cal moved toward her. His previously damp T-shirt had been replaced by a short-sleeved polo that hung up on his biceps, and she'd be willing to bet he'd showered somewhere because his dark hair curled beneath the cowboy hat, glinting clean in the sun like a new penny. He moved like a man who was accustomed to taking what he wanted. A flare of something ignited in her stomach and suddenly she couldn't take her eyes off his mouth. He had a thin upper lip, but that bottom one was so sensual. Gave her an urge to lick it, maybe bite it.

"I know, but you know what is sexy?" he asked, stopping right in front of her.

Could he hear her heart beating? Or maybe smell how turned on she was? Because she was. Like a light switch flicked. "You're defining sexy now?"

"I think we should," he said, shifting even closer. She could see the buttons on his polo had four holes. He smelled vaguely of lemon and, yeah, some kind of liniment. Even that turned her on.

He dragged one finger across her lips. And just like that, the smiles were gone. Because that was the single sexiest move she'd ever experienced. "These lips."

Maggie swallowed hard. "Uh…"

"No, don't say it," he said, running his finger lightly back across her bottom lip. "I know you think it's a bad idea to mix business and pleasure, Maggie. Thing is, I don't really care."

He slid his hand across her jaw and cupped the back of her head, his fingers tangling in the hair pulled tight in the ponytail. Tilting her head back, he studied her face.

And she studied his. Long dark eyelashes totally wasted on a man framed eyes the color of a Caribbean surf. His broad cheeks angled down and she bet his nose had been broken more than once. Lean jaw, firm chin and those damn lips she wanted to feel on her body… everywhere.

"I don't need this job, Maggie."

She inhaled deeply. "So why did you take it?"

"For this," he said, lowering his head, his lips covering hers.

4

HE HADN'T MEANT to kiss her.

But after .008 seconds he was happy as hell he did. Because kissing Maggie was like raindrops falling on the parched earth. Exactly what he needed.

She tasted like spearmint gum and sweat—an oddly potent combination.

He held her firmly, but there was no need because she didn't pull away. A soft sigh escaped against his lips as if she'd been waiting for him to do exactly what he'd done—take control of the situation. And that thought stoked his ego.

So he reached for her with his bad arm and hauled her against him, ignoring the pain because her soft body against his overshadowed the twinge in his shoulder. His hand cupped her ass, pulling her hard against him and she opened her mouth, letting him inside.

Make no mistake, Maggie could hold her own, but after a few seconds of heaven, he pulled back.

Her topaz eyes widened. "You kissed me."

He grinned. "Couldn't help myself. Those sexy lips begged me to."

"You're blaming my lips?" She swiped her hand over her mouth and stepped back. "We can't do this…uh, that. I'm your boss. You can't go around kissing your boss."

"Why not?"

"Because we have to work together. That's the first thing you learn in the corporate world."

"Do you see a corporation out here?"

"Look, I need this ranch completed so I can list it and move on with my life. I can't have you running out on me because we screw up by getting…physical."

"I wasn't planning on screwing anything up except maybe y—"

"No," she interrupted holding up a finger. "We're not going there."

But they already had. Her breathing was labored, her eyes slightly dilated and the nipples beneath the tank were hard. Her body said yes no matter what her mouth said. Her body's reaction told him all he needed to know. This would take patience. "Okay."

"Okay?" She sounded surprised.

"Yeah, okay. Now, how about that sandwich? I'm going for the turkey. No, the ham."

Maggie stared at him for a few seconds. "You can have both."

He slapped his hands together, hung his cowboy hat on the hooks inside the door and headed toward the kitchen. The living area of the Triple J had been cleared of the junk the teenagers or cats or whatever had busted windows had brought in. The furniture looked worn and stained and the whole place needed scrubbing. But it could be really nice. The fireplace was a native stone with a rustic mantel and the flooring was wood, and according to HGTV—which his mother watched with religious fervor—was desirable. All the dark molding looked intact and the horrid red paint could be changed to something tamer.

He walked into the kitchen and winced.

This would need to be gutted. Or not. Cabinets looked in good shape. Good coat of white paint would lighten them up and he could drive into the McKinney Home Depot and pick out some new stainless-steel appliances that seemed to be popular. He looked at the ugly black and white tile. That would need to go.

"The floor is ugly," Maggie said behind him.

"Just what I was thinking," he said, turning when she came inside the kitchen, looking calm and not so turned on. He was good with that because he'd tucked her earlier response to him in his back pocket. Now wasn't the time for seduction. But it would come. Maggie needed to know him better, trust him a little, before she let herself go. Cal was a patient man in many ways. It was an attribute on the tour. Be hungry but be patient. Bull riders knew timing was everything.

"I hate the idea of ripping up floors, but it will have to go. And there're some broken tiles in the master bathroom along with a cracked shower door. Whoever came here to party threw beer bottles. Not to mention the carpets in one bedroom are soiled," Maggie said.

"Soiled?"

"Someone couldn't handle his liquor."

Cal made a face. "I don't get kids these days."

Maggie snapped her finger. "You just did it."

"What?"

"Officially became old." She smiled and moved toward the refrigerator. "When you start complaining about 'kids these days,' that's when it happens. Wrinkles appear and gray hairs start pushing toward the surface."

Cal smiled. "I already have some gray." He pointed to his temples and smoothed his hair down. Definitely had hat hair.

"But that's sexy on a guy. On women?" She shook her head and started pulling out packages of lunch meat.

"I knew you thought it was sexy," he said, reaching for the paper sack sitting on the counter by the sink and pulling out the loaf of bread.

Maggie pulled out a butter knife. "You're not supposed to mention that word."

"What word?"

"Sexy."

"I never agreed to avoid it," he said, unwinding the bread tie. "I like that word 'cause it has one of my favorite things in it."

She grabbed a jar of mayonnaise from the depths of the bag along with cheese puffs and a package of Oreo cookies. "I don't see much gray."

"I'm thirty-five years old. It's there."

"You're thirty-five?"

"I'll be thirty-six in August."

"You don't look that old," she said, narrowing her eyes as if she could figure out his secret. There was no secret. He had good genes. His mother still looked like she was in her thirties and she'd turned fifty-four a few months ago. "I'm twenty-seven."

"And I thought you were older," he joked.

She narrowed her eyes at him again. This time it was in mock aggravation. "Just what a woman wants to hear—'you look old.'"

"Don't go putting words in my mouth," he teased,

opening the Cheesy-Os. "And I'll chalk it up to your sophistication and need to play by the rules."

Maggie unpeeled the slice of cheese. "Play by the rules? How's that? I canceled my return flight to stay here and clean up roach turds. I'd say that was a risky decision."

Cal had to admit it took gumption to do what Maggie was doing. Most city slickers would have put the ranch up for sale sight unseen. Washed their hands of the whole thing and taken what they could get. But Margaret Stanton had been cut from a different cloth. She saw an opportunity that with a little elbow grease and a bit of cash could become a solid basis to build a future on. Perhaps that's why he'd volunteered to help her. He admired the way she latched on to spit and polishing up the place. Or it could have been the way she filled out those shorts and halter top thing. Probably the second one but he'd still acknowledge the first.

"Sweeping up roach turds is definitely an out-of-the-box action. No cheese for me." He popped a cheese doodle into his mouth.

"You're weird. Everyone likes cheese singles."

"Not me," he said, crunching the chip. "Tastes like plastic."

"And why are you standing there watching? Open the paper plates and make yourself useful."

"That's woman's work," he joked, not moving. Instead he ate another cheese doodle and watched her dander rise.

"Don't tell me you're one of those backward idiots who still thinks it's the 1800s? I can't believe—" She snapped her mouth closed when she saw his grin. "You're intentionally ruffling my feathers."

"I like to watch your face get red. And you start breathing hard which draws my eyes to your chest." He looked pointedly at her breasts.

"You're a pervert," she said, slapping cheese onto both the sandwiches like that would teach him to mess with her.

"It will only get worse," he said, pulling the package of paper plates out of the bag from the Stop-N-Go, Coyote Creek's finest in gas-station grocers.

Maggie snorted and slathered the bread with mayonnaise, not even bothering to ask him if he liked it on his sandwich. He did, but she didn't know that. This sandwich was a lesson to a man who stroked a cat the wrong way. She smushed the two pieces of bread together and grabbed a plate from his hands. The action struck him as domestic, and for a brief second he wondered what it would be like to have a woman smarting off to him in the kitchen every night. What it would be like to have the elusive family he'd once dreamed about as a child when his mother was working late and he lay in the twin bed made with threadbare sheets his mother had brought home from the motel. What would it be like to live somewhere other than his trailer or hotel rooms with another cowboy snoring in the adjacent bed? What would it be like to have a place to belong?

But as soon as the thought flitted through his mind, he chased it away.

Real cowboys didn't have families or worry about crown molding and rain showerheads. Oh, sure, some of the guys he knew had wives and kids, but even they found comfort in Jim Beam and a soft body when they were on the road. It was the cowboy way. Charlie had been wrong about a lot of things, but when he told Cal cowboys didn't do well strapped down, he wasn't lying. Cal knew that firsthand. His own father had been a cowboy, hadn't he? And where was he?

Cal knew who and what he was. Standing in the dated, dusty kitchen of the Triple J was a lark, something he did only because he was bored and wanted to be with Maggie. By mid-August he'd be in Mobile at the first event on the second leg. And Maggie would be back on the East Coast, hopefully a fine memory for him. If she played nice.

"Here," she said, jabbing the paper plate with the lonely sandwich on it toward him.

"Thanks. You got a beer or something?" he asked, loading the plate with half the Cheesy-Os.

"No."

"You want one? I can run out to my trailer."

She shrugged. "When in Texas."

"Right," he said, toasting her with a cheese doodle.

AFTER THE SANDWICH SUPPER, Maggie pulled out what was left of the dinnerware and filled the sink with soapy water. Some of the pieces had been broken by the kids who'd busted in the back door so they could party. She'd put in a call to the sheriff's office regarding the vandalism, but they'd told her Charlie had already filed a complaint and they'd investigated to no avail. But they would send deputies by for the next week or so until word got out that the Triple J was now occupied. Deputy Riser felt sure that the occupancy would eliminate the ranch as a go-to party zone.

Cal sat at the table, frowning at his phone. "Signal's crap."

"Well, since you can't play on your phone, you can dry," she said, tossing him a drying cloth.

"Hey, I'm an eight-to-five guy. I'm off."

"Pay for your dinner," she said, setting a stack of plates into the dishwater.

"That means I have to dry only one plate. Maybe a cup." But she heard the chair scrape against the floor. He moved behind her, prickling her nerve ends, making her want to lean back and feel him pressed to her.

That kiss.

That kiss had been so good. Like the first lick of mint chocolate chip ice cream. But going there was walking a tightrope and if there was one thing she didn't need at the moment, it was a combustible relationship turning sour in the ninth inning. She needed this place fixed up and ready to sell. That meant she needed Cal to stay focused on the job she'd hired him to do. No hanky-panky, no matter how incredible he kissed or how much she loved his aw-shucks sexiness. "So tell me about bull riding. How'd you get started?"

"When I was ten years old, my mom won tickets off the radio to a PRCA event in Fort Worth. All of it was exciting—roping, bronc bustin' and even the barrel events. But when the end rolled around and those bulls hit the chute, I felt something electric. I'll never forget the way my stomach dropped when that gate opened and that cowboy rode that big sucker. I decided right then and there, I wanted to do that."

"But it's so dangerous."

"That's part of it. It ain't just holding on. It's riding. There's a difference. And when you can hit that zone, when you know what the bull is going to do because it's there in your bones, there's nothing like it. Maybe it's like getting high or something. I don't know. But it's indescribable."

His words carried a reverence. She could tell he loved climbing onto a snorting, huge monster. "So don't you win a buckle or something? How many have you won?"

Cal smiled and took the soapy plate from her. "I've won a few."

"You don't want to talk about it, huh? Is it the injury?"

"No," he said, his lower lip curving.

He had nice lips that knew their way around. Probably all those women who showed up at the corrals—what did they call them again? She couldn't remember. "Then what?"

"I don't know. I'm taking a break from all that right now. Trying to heal and get my mind right. Guess I don't feel like talking about the bulls and the buckles and the—"

"Bunnies?" she said, finally remembering the name that escaped her. "I've heard that term before."

Cal looked over at her. "Them, too."

Something ugly moved inside her. She didn't like the idea of faceless women in shiny halter tops and boots kissing his boo-boos better. Which was strange because she had no stake in Cal. He was a guy who'd done her a solid a few days ago, a guy she'd hired for a job, and pretty much the one person in Texas she could count on. Who he screwed or didn't screw shouldn't bother her.

But it did.

She peered out into the Texas night through a window that needed serious cleaning as she scrubbed the dishes. The dishwasher was already full of the cookware and silverware. Thankfully it had worked, as had the dried-up chunk of dish-washing detergent she'd pried out of the Cascade box under the sink. Cal remained silent, taking the plates she handed to him, drying and stacking them in a pile on the counter.

The whole scene felt strange and yet oddly comforting.

So much inside her twisted like a tornado. Everything had proved easier said than done. Her secret hope of finding a perfect place to land had been washed down the drain. Not that she had actually truly entertained the idea of moving to the middle of Nowhere, Texas. Probably had internalized all those stories Bud had told her about life in Texas and created a fairy-tale ideal or something. Like the faraway castle every little girl dreamed of. Or maybe it was she hated the thought of giving any of Bud's selfish, whiny children part of the proceeds. Or maybe she had merely hoped things would be easier than they were. That she would have driven up to the Triple J, fallen in love with her new home and found a million dollars buried in the backyard. She had wanted to feel something for this place.

But she hadn't. Not really.

Instead it felt like a big pain in the ass and now her life was on pause.

But perhaps being stuck on pause wasn't a bad thing. Maybe she needed to take time to think about what her future held. For many years she'd been on autopilot, taking care of Bud's affairs, balancing work and merely existing. Not much passion in her life and not much time to study the stars, wash a dish and listen to the absolute quiet of the night.

She'd just pulled the drain plug when a pair of headlights swept over the barn.

"Cal," she whispered. "Look."

He leaned over, his shoulder brushing against hers. "Shit."

"What do we do?"

"We run their asses out of here is what we do," he said, tossing the towel and heading toward the screened door.

"Wait, what if they have a gun or something?"

"They're local punks. I used to be one. I know how to deal with them," he said, pushing out the door. She saw the headlights cut off. The truck had parked right by the pens.

Maggie followed Cal, squinting to adjust to the darkness. The sun had gone to bed thirty minutes ago and already it was pitch-black with only the stars above giving weak light. The bulbs in the outside lights had been busted. Cal had replacement bulbs on the huge list for the Home Depot, but that didn't help since Maggie couldn't see her surroundings. She picked her way around a big bush on the side of the house, noting Cal had slowed and walked calmly toward the pickup.

Truck doors opened and two shapes emerged—a guy and a girl.

Maggie caught the glint of golden hair and could see the boy held a bottle of liquor. The girl squealed when the boy grabbed her and lifted her. She wrapped her legs around his waist, giggling. They started kissing and at that moment, Maggie's mind flashed to the spent condoms she'd found in the master bedroom. Yeah, there were a lot of them.

"Hey," Cal shouted.

The couple froze and then the boy said, "Oh, fuck." He dropped the girl and the booze before scrambling back toward the driver's door. The girl screeched and ran toward the passenger side. The light came on in the truck and Maggie could plainly see two teenagers—a boy with shaggy dark hair, the girl with long blond hair. They looked panicked. Totally busted.

"Stop," Cal yelled, running toward the pickup. The headlights came on as the engine roared to life. Cal grabbed the door handle as the kid shifted into Reverse. "Goddamn it. Stop."

"Cal?" the kid shouted.

The truck slammed into Park, rocking the vehicle.

"Get the hell out," Cal growled, cradling his bad shoulder, a grimace of pain evident in the light given off by the headlights.

"Shit, man, what are you doing out here?" the kid said, opening the door. The light in the cab came on again and Maggie could see the boy more distinctly. It was obvious Cal knew the kid.

Cal hauled him out of the truck. "What in God's name are you doing out here? This is private property."

"Nothing. I mean, me and Hannah were just, you know, um, making out and stuff. Everyone comes out here for that," the kid said, scrambling to pull away from the grip Cal had on his arm. The blonde girl started crying.

Maggie finally reached the truck. The kid looked at her and then looked back at Cal. "What are you doing here? Who's she?"

"I'm Margaret Stanton, the owner of the Triple J."

"The owner?" the kid repeated, suddenly looking scared. "No one ever said someone owned this place. Everyone thinks it's abandoned."

Cal let go of the kid. "Maggie, this is Wyatt. My dumb-ass brother."

"You have a brother?"

"Yeah, a brother who engages in criminal activity like breaking and entering. Should we add vandalism?"

Wyatt snapped his head up. "Everyone comes out here."

"And trashes property that doesn't belong to them? Is that what's cool these days? Vandalism? Tearing up—"

"I didn't do none of this," Wyatt said, anger seeping into his voice. Cal's brother was several inches taller than him, but still slim as a fence post. He had the same color hair, but he seemed to have brown eyes and a swarthy complexion. "People tore this place up a long time ago."

"You may not be destroying property, but you *are* trespassing."

"Well, I didn't know. We were just looking for a place to—"

"Just shut up, Wyatt," the blonde said, wiping the tears leaking from her eyes.

Maggie placed a hand on Cal's arm. She could feel his frustration. "It's okay, Cal."

"It's not okay. These kids have been—"

"Cal," she said, rubbing his arm. Wyatt noticed and looked at her a bit harder, so she turned to him. "Wyatt, I'd appreciate if you'd let everyone know the Triple J is occupied. We're renovating the property and there will be a lot of workers around in the next few weeks. The property will be sold to new owners who won't look favorably on local kids tearing up their things. As of tonight, the Triple J is closed for drinking, carousing and, uh, making out. Tell everyone to find a new place to party."

Wyatt nodded. "Okay, but you're not going to, like, press charges or something, right? I mean, we didn't do any graffiti or anything."

"No charges. And now you can put it on blast." Cal uncrossed his arms.

"No one says that anymore," Wyatt observed.

"Well, whatever kids call it these days," Cal said, nodding toward the cab. "Take Hannah home. I won't say anything to Mom about this. Wait, have you been drinking?"

"Not yet," Wyatt said, looking disappointed his night hadn't gone as planned. "But if we had, this would have totally killed our buzz."

"I better not catch you drinking and driving. I'll go to Gary and you can kiss your 4x4 goodbye." Cal set his hands on his hips, looking commanding. Maggie noted how good commanding looked on him.

"Way to be a bro," Wyatt muttered before pausing. "Wait, why are you out here, anyway?"

"I'm helping Maggie get the place ready to go on the block," Cal said.

"You?" Wyatt looked at his older brother like he'd just announced he was wearing panty hose and a bra. "I thought you were about to start training. Does Mom know?"

"She knows and I'm still training. Now take Hannah home."

Wyatt shrugged, his dark eyes reflecting amusement. "I guess I ain't blind and can see what you're up to."

Cal didn't look too happy about his younger brother's parting shot. Wyatt climbed into the truck, shut the door and fired the engine, giving his brother a salute on the way out.

"What does he think you're up to?" Maggie said, watching the twin red brake lights as they blinked in the darkness before disappearing over the rise.

"Let's just say the apple doesn't fall far from the tree," Cal said, turning back toward the house. The inky darkness settled around them again, the night eerily quiet other than the serenade of crickets.

So he thought their kiss was the beginning. But she had the power to nip the attraction in the bud if she so wished. Problem was…she wasn't sure she wished it.

5

THREE DAYS LATER Cal pulled into the parking lot of the Home Depot and turned to Maggie. The woman wore a sundress that gathered just beneath her full breasts and strappy sandals that would do little good in a home-improvement store. But he had to admit she looked delicious.

Practical or sexy?

He'd go with sexy every time. Or at least most times. A woman like Maggie made him glad to be a man.

"So I have the list right here," she said, unbuckling and waving the pad he'd been scribbling on for the past few days. "Where shall we start?"

"At the top," he said, climbing from the cab and jogging around to get her door. She'd been in the process of opening it and looked at him oddly when he pulled it open and held out his hand. "I'm helping you down."

"Why?"

He sighed. "Bud wasn't much of a Texan, was he?"

"He was from Philly. Texas was his hobby. Though he often commented on how much he wished he'd sold the business and moved down here full-time. Guess Edelman's Ice Cream was part of who he was. Couldn't let something his father loved go so easily."

"I was referring to his manners. Didn't he ever open a door for a lady?"

Maggie stopped next to the orange shopping carts and tilted her head. Real cute-like. "I get that dudes down here think they have to be chivalrous, but women are perfectly capable of opening a damn door."

"You don't get it," he said, shaking his head, moving toward the double doors that swooshed open, giving him the scent of fresh lumber.

"Nope, but I'll try to appreciate it better," she said, grabbing a shopping cart.

"Perfect. We need some doorknobs," he said, grabbing a few pewter-colored ones from a display near the machine that made keys. Counting out five, he set them in the back of the cart.

"Those aren't at the top of the list. Are those the right size?" she asked, eyeing the packages.

"Cal Lincoln?" the voice came from his left, making his heart sink. He'd hoped he could get through the afternoon without the PBR faithful recognizing him. Which is why he'd left his jeans and boots at home, choosing the seldom-used athletic shorts and sneakers instead. He felt naked without his cowboy hat, but compromised by jerking on a Nike visor. He looked like a suburban soccer dad. Or so he'd thought.

He turned and donned a smile.

"Damn, man, I haven't seen you in eight or nine years, but I recognized that walk," the man said, holding out his hand.

Cal grabbed it, staring at the man hard, trying to figure out if he was supposed to know him or if he was a fan. The man looked about his age though he had balded prematurely. A round basketball stomach made the Texas Rangers T-shirt stick out and when the Lord was handing out asses, this man had skipped the line. But the friendly smile was familiar. "Hey, man."

"You don't remember me, huh?" the guy said, taking his hand.

"You got me there. See so many people—"

"James Maloney?"

"Oh, shit, man. Of course. Coyote Creek High School. Can't believe I didn't recognize you," Cal said, slapping him on the shoulder. James had been a baseball teammate before Cal had dropped out to pursue bull riding full-time. Of course his friend had had a thick mane of curly hair back then.

James ran a hand over his shining head. "Well, I've lost a little up top." He looked at Maggie with an appreciative smile, unasked question in his eyes.

"I'm Maggie," she said, holding out her hand. "I'm Cal's boss."

She liked saying that. And that amused Cal. James frowned, but managed to recoup the smile. "His boss, huh? Y'all married or something?"

"Of course not. He's *working* for me," she said, dropping his hand.

James shot Cal a funny look. "I thought you were rehabbing the shoulder?"

"Oh, he still goes to physical therapy several times a week," Maggie said, glancing at him with a questioning look as if she didn't understand how a guy he hadn't seen in ten years would know he was in rehab. He supposed she was so accustomed to speaking for Bud Edelman, she naturally tried to handle situations. Like the night before last with his brother. She'd inserted herself right in the middle of the issue, even stroking his arm to calm him when she felt him losing his temper. Underneath her calm, cool vibe was a nosy, bossy busybody, but Cal appreciated she was a little big for her britches. And if he could get her out of those britches? Even better.

"Well, it's nice to meet you, Maggie the boss." James gave her an amused look. She narrowed her eyes.

"I'll be seeing you, man," Cal said, slapping his old friend on the back again. "Gotta get back to work before my boss docks my pay."

James laughed. "Yeah, me, too. My wife's been texting me to get my behind out to the garden center for the last few minutes. Total ball buster." And with a final wave, James disappeared behind a display of shop vacuums.

Cal took the list from the cart and peered at it. "Okay, let's head over to grab the caulk I'll need for the sink and bathtub." He started walking, but after a few yards he sensed she wasn't behind him. Figured she wouldn't follow him.

Turning, he found her regarding him.

"What?"

She shoved the cart to the side and walked toward him, arms crossed. She reminded him of his mother when he'd spilled something on the clean kitchen floor. "Something's not gelling with you. Everyone knows you're rehabbing your shoulder. At first I thought it was because Coyote Creek is such a small town, but now this guy you haven't seen in ten years knows about it."

"What if I'm on Facebook?"

She wagged a finger. "Nuh-uh, you would have recognized your friend. Would have known he'd gone bald. So what aren't you telling me?"

At that moment a store associate in an orange vest passed them. Then she stopped and backed up. "Cal Lincoln?"

He donned the smile he put on each week when he stayed hours after the last ride to sign autographs for PBR fans. "Hey."

"Oh. My. God." The woman slapped her palms together and then emitted a high-pitched squeal that dogs three counties over could probably hear. "You're my rider. You're my rider!"

"Thank you," he said, stretching out his hand just as a shopping cart slammed into his ass. He turned to find Maggie glaring at him.

"Sally," the woman said grabbing his hand and pumping it up and down. "Oh, crap. I gotta get you to sign something. My son loves you. He even has a T-shirt with you on it. Wore it every Friday to school last year."

"Here," Maggie said, ripping off a piece of the yellow notebook paper and setting it over the list. "And here's a pen so Cal can sign something for your son. For what? I don't exactly know."

Sally made an incredulous face. "You're joking, right?"

"Not at all."

Sally looked at him like Maggie was cracked. He shrugged and arched an eyebrow. "What's your boy's name?"

"Ryan. He's seven years old. You're his hero. Well, you and John Cena."

"Good taste," Cal cracked, scribbling a signature to the woman's son.

"Oh, and would you mind taking a picture with me?" she asked, digging her cell phone out of her apron pocket. She handed it to Maggie. "If you don't mind?"

"Of course not," Maggie said, taking the phone and holding it up. Clicking the button, she took three photos and handed the phone back. After a few more seconds of Sally fawning on him, he started toward the back of the store. Normally, he didn't have to worry about being recognized by fans. Oh, sure, every now and then someone recognized him, but usually he flew under the radar of even the most loyal of fans. But he was in Texas only thirty minutes from where he rode his first bull. People followed him avidly on the PBR tour around these parts. He heard Maggie behind him, pushing the cart with the wonky wheel.

She bore down on him like a field sergeant.

Finally he stopped in front of a collection of storm doors.

"That woman got your autograph, took a picture with you and called you her rider. You're good at bull riding, aren't you?"

"Two-time world champion."

"Holy crap," she mused, folding her arms over her chest again…which sucked because he liked the view of her rack. "You didn't need this job. Why'd you take it?"

"I was bored." Probably not a good answer. But it was the truth.

"Bored? You took a job helping me because you were bored? That's insane."

"I climb onto the back of two-thousand pound animals that could stomp a mud hole in me. I'm a little crazy."

Maggie actually looked hurt. "Is this about the flirting? The kiss? Was this about getting a piece of ass?"

"Maybe."

Her eyes widened. "Seriously? You admit it?"

He looked for the section that housed the ladders because the hole he'd dug had gotten deep as hell. "Look, this isn't just about sex, okay? Yeah. I want you. I'll be honest. I've been home for six weeks. Three of them were miserable as hell with my mother constantly in my ear about crap. This last wreck has her convinced I have a death wish. And I hurt like a son of a bitch. But when you walked into that diner, it was like a big ol' glass of water set in front of a thirsty man. I had to take a drink... or try to."

Maggie didn't respond for a few seconds. Instead she studied him under the harsh lighting, framed against the prefabricated doors. "You could have asked me out to dinner. That's the normal way a man goes about pursuing a woman."

"But you needed help."

"And you wanted to fix things for me?"

"Maybe a little. I felt bad for you and as I mentioned, I've been without much to occupy my time. My shoulder's good enough to hold a paintbrush and hammer some nails. I need to get stronger and drop some pounds. There's only so much I can do in a gym." He dropped his gaze, taking in her tight body in the sundress and the toes he'd thought about nibbling. "And the scenery wasn't bad."

"I feel like an idiot. When you told me you lived in a trailer on your mother's property—"

"You thought I was a loser? Didn't have a job and lived with Mommy, huh?" He cracked a smile. But he had to admit, it would be easy to jump to that conclusion. He had been hanging out in a diner at 9:00 a.m. on a weekday. And he'd eagerly suggested he could help her with the ranch.

"So why didn't you tell me you were, like, some celebrity bull rider?"

"You didn't ask."

"I'm asking now. What else? Do you have a girlfriend? A…wife?" Her mouth tightened.

"No. The last girl I dated seriously was in college. The only other thing I can think of to tell you is I'm currently ranked fourth, my nickname is Hollywood, I modeled in a Hugo Boss ad, and if you hear something about an orgy in Denver, I was *not* there. No matter what anyone says." He spread his hands out and hoped she didn't start hurling the doorknobs still sitting in the cart at him.

Maggie gave an ironic laugh. "Oh, is that all?"

"Yep. I've totally come clean."

She picked up the list with a heavy sigh. "If someone would have told me I'd be standing in a Home Depot in McKinney, Texas, with a guy who models Hugo Boss underwear, I'd tell them they'd been smoking some bad shit."

"It wasn't underwear," he said, taking the shopping cart. "It was a suit. But I wore my gold buckle."

Maggie merely shook her head and fell in step behind him. "Okay, Hollywood, let's get this list completed so we can get back and cure your boredom."

"Oh, really?" he asked, wiggling his eyebrows. "What did you have in mind? Because the lubricant aisle is right over there." He pointed toward aisle five. He had no clue what was in aisle five. He just wanted Maggie to smile again. To maybe consider getting naked with him at some point.

"But I need caulk," she said. Though she made it sound dirty.

Like maybe he didn't need that ladder, after all.

6

MAGGIE SNITCHED ONE of Cal's French fries from the Burger Boy bag and slid another look at him as he drove through the intersection.

Two-time world champion, huh?

Not such a loser, after all.

Okay, she'd never thought him a loser. She'd wondered why he lived with his mother and didn't seem to have a job, but she'd never judged him. Humble beginnings were her middle name so she never looked down or up on the social ladder…though she was constantly aware. Paid to be aware of one's surroundings. It had helped her to navigate a gilded world of charity dinners and boardrooms with Bud. She knew firsthand the rungs were often broken or slick.

But she'd never imagined Cal would have people calling him "their" rider…and wanting autographs…and knowing his rehab schedule. So strange. And somehow so intriguing. She'd been attracted to him before she knew he was a rodeo rock star, but now she couldn't stop looking at him. Of course, that might make her shallow. Or merely honest with herself. After all, most women preferred a hot successful guy over a hot unemployed one still living with Mama.

She swiped another fry.

"Hey, lay off my fries, woman," Cal said, making another turn, taking them farther from the center of the small city. "You better not eat them all before we get there."

"Get where?"

"You'll see."

Ten minutes later, after a bone-jarring ride over a rutted dirt road, they emerged into a clearing beside a small lake. The sun glittered off the waves. Thick grass and small trees crowded the banks. "A lake?"

"A picnic," he said, lifting the bag of food from between them and opening the door. The hot Texas wind blew inside the cab, urging her out. She obliged, sliding down to the yellowed grass waving against the running board.

Cal had angled the truck parallel to the lake and lowered the tailgate, creating a bench for them. All of the supplies they'd bought at Home Depot were piled into the back, held with several bungee cords. There was just enough room for both of them to sit, legs dangling over the edge of the tailgate. Above them birds hopped along the branches of the large oak tree.

"It's nice out here," she said, digging her grilled chicken salad from the depths of the bag, handing him the cheeseburger he'd ordered, swiping another fry in the process. "How'd you find it?"

"I dated a girl from McKinney in high school. We came here to make out."

"Of course you did."

"What? Don't tell me you didn't have a favorite make-out spot back in Philly."

"I didn't," she said, shaking her head and then using her teeth to rip off the tab for the fat-free dressing. "I lived at Briarcliff my whole life. My mom and I had a garage apartment and there wasn't really a place for making out. Though I did kiss the gardener's nephew in the gazebo once. Didn't last long. He was only there for a weeklong visit. So no nooky on the estate."

"Why'd you have a garage apartment?" he asked, biting into his burger and looking way happier than she could stabbing the cellulose lettuce and pretending her salad was delish. His hair ruffled in the breeze and the visor made him look sporty…masculine…sexy.

"My mother was Bud's housekeeper, so we lived at Briarcliff—that's the name Bud's ex-wife, Phyllis, gave the estate. Outside of the four years I spent at college, it's been home. I can't complain, though, because it was a beautiful place to grow up. There were stables, a tennis court and a pool. I used those things whenever I wanted. Well, at least after Phyllis divorced Bud. I was nine years old when they split. Their kids were grown so I didn't have to worry about waiting until no one was using the pool for a pool party."

"And your father?"

Maggie shrugged. "I don't have a father."

He jerked his gaze on her, making her feel naked… and not in a good way. "What do you mean?"

"Well, my conception was a one-night thing that happened when my mother was young. The Edelmans used to have big parties and, honestly, I'm not sure my mother knows who my father is. I know it's weird, but I truly never missed out on having a father figure. I had the gardener, the horse trainer and even Bud."

Cal's eyes narrowed. "But it doesn't bother you not knowing?"

"Maybe a bit, but I had a good mother and a happy upbringing."

"Well, that's something," he acknowledged with a nod.

"So what about your father? You never mentioned him."

Cal looked away. "Because he's not worth talking about."

Maggie popped a smashed grape tomato into her mouth and chewed. She might not have daddy issues, but she could see Cal did. "I'm sorry if my attitude about my father came off as flippant. Plenty of kids out there don't have anyone to love them, so I was glad I had my mom…and Bud to a degree. He was a mentor, always there when I needed him."

"He left us when I was a month old," Cal said.

"That's awful. Do you know where he is?" she asked, setting her hand on his thigh.

"Probably working a spread up in Montana or Utah. He calls about once a year. Sometimes I answer. He's proud of me. That's what he likes to say, but that's all he has to offer. If I weren't winning big, he'd never call," Cal said.

"I'm sorry," she said, hearing the anger in his voice. She'd never known her father—no name and no face— so she didn't have to miss him. Obviously, Cal resented the man who'd thrown him away. For good reason.

"Don't be. He lost the chance to be my father a long time ago. He was the sperm donor, like your dad." He wadded up the wrapper and tossed it into the bag before shoving several fries into his mouth. "Can we drop this conversation? I like talking to you, but not about my family. Or the PBR. Or...let's go ahead and rule out terrorism, gay marriage and anything to do with reality television, okay?"

"Jeez, what's left to talk about?" she joked, still reeling from the revelation they both lacked fathers in their lives. Talk about two peas in a pod.

"How about the fact I can't take my eyes off you?" he said. Case in point, his gaze was on her, traveling down to the stretchy top of the sundress.

"I bet you say that to all your bosses." She laughed, even as she felt desire stir inside her.

"I've never worked for anyone who looked like you... for anyone who made me want to lick my way up her neck."

"Yeah, that probably would have landed you in the dirt with a black eye," she said, chasing an olive around the tasteless dressing. She should have splurged on a cheeseburger like Cal had, but she was so accustomed to making the wise decision in her life that she hadn't thought twice about how nice a juicy burger covered with American cheese would taste.

Cal shoved the paper bag to the side and took the tray she'd been holding and set it aside. "You're finished with that, right?"

"I guess I am now," she said, tossing her fork into the depths of the below-par salad. She wasn't hungry any longer. At least not for food.

Cal leaned into her, tucking a strand of hair behind her ear. "So since we're being so honest on this little trip into town, let's talk turkey."

"Turkey, huh?"

"Yeah, 'cause I want you. And you want me."

"Or so you think."

His teeth flashed white against his tanned skin. Amused by her. Like a cat playing with a mouse he'd cornered. That thought made her tingly. Excited.

"Oh, you want me, *baby*. You're trying to tell yourself that you shouldn't indulge." He looked back at the half-eaten salad sitting on the tailgate.

"Or maybe I know you're not good for me. That you'd make me fat." Keeping a barrier between them had seemed so important, but now she wondered if she'd been deluding herself. A woman didn't run from the kind of want that rose inside of her. It wasn't going away.

"Oh, baby. I won't make you fat," he said, tracing her bottom lip with a finger.

"You won't?" she whispered, wanting to believe him.

"I'll make you a lot of things, but fat won't be one of them." He set a hand on her hip, drawing her around so she faced him. His breath was as hot as the wind tangling her hair. She could smell the mixture of Irish Spring soap and a unique scent that was decidedly male. Intoxicating. "What will you make me?"

"Tired." He kissed her bare shoulder.

"Sweaty." And the sensitive spot behind her ear.

"Satisfied." Then his lips captured hers. And it was good. So, so good.

Maggie couldn't help herself. She leaned in and kissed him back. Tongues met and she sighed against his lips as she tasted French fries. Not cellulose lettuce and crappy ranch dressing. But hot, delicious, very-bad-for-you goodness that embodied everything Cal Lincoln was.

Cal cradled her jaw, angling her head so he could take the kiss deeper. A curl of heat unfurled in her stomach, blanketing her like Texas humidity. The sweet desire absent for the past few years latched onto her, sank its teeth into her.

Somehow one of her hands found its way to his stomach, sliding over the soft cotton, as she reveled in the hard male beneath. Making a little mewling sound deep in her throat, she allowed her hand to drop down to the elastic waistband of his shorts.

Cal broke the kiss, his gaze probing her eyes. "We both need this."

His words were meant to confirm, but instead doubt threatened her desire. She needed lots of things—a new career, a quick sale of the ranch and probably a pair of cowboy boots, thanks to that snake. But hot sweaty sex with Cal could be Dangerous with a capital *D*. She didn't need dangerous or complicated.

"But we shouldn't," she said, pulling her hand back into her lap, knowing she sounded halfhearted. "We're both at a weird place right now. You with your shoulder. Me with this whole ranch thing. Sex could make things more complicated."

Cal raised his eyebrows. "I see. Another control issue?"

"Making good decisions is not trying to control everything or everyone."

"What you see as complicated, I see as simple. There's no downside to me and you having good old-fashioned naked fun."

"I'm not the kind of girl a man has fun with, naked or otherwise," she said, wanting to believe that about herself. Lord knew she'd used that line several times before. She wasn't like other girls. She didn't do one-night stands or booty calls. She dated the right way—dinner, movies and maybe a good-night kiss with no tongue. Cal Lincoln made her want to break all the rules. He made her want to straddle him right there on the tailgate. To hell with the unwritten rules of dating.

Of course, Maggie knew the reason she'd always been careful when it came to men—her mother's experience. Her mother had been young when she went to work for the Edelmans and she'd obviously bumbled into something she couldn't handle one weekend. The result of tossing out the unwritten rules had cried for 2:00 a.m. feedings. So it was only natural Maggie grew up trying to make the right decisions all the time. Cal Lincoln wasn't the right decision. He was a bored cowboy looking to pass some time before he took off again. And whether he needed the job or not, he worked for her. Too many arrows pointed away from him. Only one pointed toward him. Being horny was no good reason to jump into something that could make the shaky ground beneath her crack.

Cal traced a finger over her shoulder. "Just because I want to bend you over this tailgate and make you scream doesn't mean I don't respect you."

She snorted, pulling away. "Some would say that's an oxymoron."

"Some don't understand how mature adults play. Think about it this way. We have a little over a month until I leave for Mobile and you put the ranch on the block and head back east. Game over. But until we get there, we could have weeks of laughter, good sex and companionship."

He made it sound so simple.

"Plus, since we know we're done in August, we don't have to go through the cold silence, nasty fights and a hurtful breakup. We'll have good, dirty fun between the sheets, on the new kitchen countertops…in that new shower we'll put in."

Maggie squeezed her eyes shut as if she could shut out the images of their two bodies slick with sweat wrapped round each other. She knew it would be amazing between them and it had been so long since she'd made love with someone. A cute pink vibrator and erotica were a poor substitute for the scrape of a beard against her nipples, the weight of a man on her, and the mind-bending orgasm achieved as he went hard and deep. But…

Cal slid off the tailgate and walked to the trunk of the oak tree, giving her room physically and figuratively. He turned toward her. "I'm not going to beg you, Maggie. I respect a woman's right to choose for herself what she wants in a relationship. I could use cheap seduction tactics, but I won't. You like to make logical decisions, so I'll leave it to you. I've pretty much made my case for a no-strings-attached, mutually beneficial relationship."

Maggie slid off the tailgate, grabbing a leaf dangling from the branch above her head. "You think it will be that easy? A clean break? No mess?"

Cal shrugged. "Neither of us is at a place for anything more. We'll have a few laughs and leave with a good memory."

She couldn't deny his argument sounded logical. Eliminating the messiness of a breakup and setting guidelines meant they'd both know the score. No shaky ground…just hot, gratifying sex. When she left Texas, she'd be ready to start a new life and perhaps being with a hot cowboy could make that easier. She'd feel more confident, less needy and most important, sexually fulfilled. Or at least she assumed he was as advertised. "You know, from the moment I first arrived in Coyote Creek, I've been off balance. I made the decision to remodel the ranch and hire you without much forethought which is highly atypical of me. I can't say I've been very practical about the path I've chosen for the next month or so. Maybe that's a good thing. Maybe I need a little spontaneity. Maybe I need some…hot sex?"

A smile curved Cal's lips. "You need sexual healing."

"Not if you're going to start singing that song or making doctor jokes about delivering the medicine," she joked, feeling herself go over the edge of reason. But she'd enjoy the fall…and according to Cal, there'd never be a splat. This wasn't a bad decision. It was inevitable. They'd been moving toward this. Why stop?

Cal reached out and took her hand, bringing her to him. She let him. "Your answer is…?"

Maggie lifted onto her toes and looped her arms around his neck. "Take me home, unpack the truck because we can't risk any high school kids showing up to plunder the supplies and then screw my brains out."

Cal dropped a kiss on her lips. "But I like your brains, boss lady."

Maggie pulled his head back down to hers and bit his lower lip. "The brains can stay as long as the screwing takes place."

"Can I negotiate a bonus for a job well done?"

Maggie slid her hand down his stomach and clasped the hardness jutting against her belly. "I see a real possibility of a bonus."

Cal closed his eyes before pulling the keys out of his pocket. "Let's go. Now."

Laughter and sweet anticipation rose in her. "In a hurry, are you? I thought I'd finish my salad."

"The hell you will," he said, pushing her toward the truck, making her laugh. "You said I should have asked you out to dinner. Well, that was it. Let's move on to the after-date stuff."

"You call eating a salad on a tailgate taking me on a date?" she teased, but she followed.

"No, that was a second date. I'm counting the ham-and-turkey sandwich as the first one," he said, climbing into the truck, looking back at her to order, "Hurry up, boss."

7

THE SUN HAD slipped from the western sky, leaving streaks of lavender on the horizon. Crickets came out to play and the lonely hoot of a barn owl accompanied the creak of the back screen door as Cal stepped into the kitchen for the date Maggie had insisted on. The aroma of something saucy hit him along with the sight of Maggie wearing an apron and a pair of short denim cutoffs. She looked good standing there with the sweet curve of her ass nearly showing and a wooden spoon in hand. She sang a Beyoncé song about who runs the world at the top of her lungs.

Hours before, he'd driven back to the Triple J like a bat out of hell, intent on getting Maggie into bed. But on arrival, he had to address some issues with the paint crew and pay the roofers who'd put a new roof on in only a day's time. Maggie had given him a smile full of promise before disappearing into the house, leaving him to unload the supplies. He'd discovered Charlie had fixed the pen and left, miracle of miracles. Then after looking over some fencing that needed to be replaced and calling an electrician to come out and check the wiring in the barn, he'd finally managed to answer the emails that had stacked up and make a call to Dr. Tubby McCoy, the PBR physician, to discuss the exam he'd undergo in Mobile. A call to his agent imparted the news Hugo Boss wanted him to do a public appearance at some fashion thing in Paris. Probably wouldn't make that with the world championship on the line, but he'd never been to France or feted by a designer. Could be fun. And he'd ordered a bucking barrel to be installed in the barn so he could start practicing. Once he got comfortable there, he'd see about going to local rodeos and getting some actual rides. August was bearing down on him…but until then, he had Maggie.

She whirled at the sound of the door shutting. "Oh, you scared me."

He smiled, loving that she'd left her dark brown hair to curl softly over her shoulders. The white T-shirt clung tightly to her curves and with her feet in flip-flops, she looked far removed from the woman who'd walked into the Barbwire diner last week. Gone was the cool professional, and in her place was a warm, willing woman with a smoking body. His gaze slid over the flare of her hips, the tight rack and those porn-star lips that drove him crazy. "You're a terrible singer."

Her face was flushed, maybe from the heat of the stove or the anticipation thrumming between them like a hive full of honeybees. "I know. I think a wolf howled during the first verse."

"Not wolf. Coyote maybe." Cal walked over and pulled her into his arms, loving how she fit him. He dipped his head and found she tasted like red sauce. "Mmm, you taste—"

"—like garlic?" she interrupted.

"Maybe a little, but if—" he took the spoon and scooped a taste out of the pot "—I have some, too, it won't matter."

"I should have fixed something else," she said with a sigh, wiping her hands on the apron. "It's our first real date and I go with Italian. But I make a good marinara sauce. Wanted to impress you."

"Been a long time since someone cared to impress me with cooking skills."

"Your mother doesn't cook for you when you're home?"

"Ruth sucks in the kitchen. She spent too many days cleaning up after other people to want to clean the kitchen nightly."

"Your mother was a housekeeper, too?"

"At the Coyote Creek Motel." When he was younger he'd been ashamed of having a mother who was a maid, of living such a scrubby existence, but now he understood how his mother's work ethic and determination had molded him. His mother had gone from maid to manager. And then she'd met Gary Whitehorse, a wealthy cattleman and businessman, whom she married. Needless to say, his mother hadn't cleaned a toilet in seventeen years.

"Something else we have in common—hardworking single mothers who had to make other people's beds," she said, adding a splash of red wine to the sauce and stirring. He reached past her and grabbed the glass of wine sitting on the counter beside her and took a sip.

She wrinkled her cute nose. "I hate drinking from the same glass after other people."

He swallowed the wine, noting the spicy hint of black pepper paired with currant and jam. Yeah, he loved wine, not that anyone would believe a dumb bull rider had discerning tastes. "Really? 'Cause you're about to get all up in this." He waved his hands around his face.

"You really know how to romance a girl, don't you?" She snorted, pulling on oven mitts and lifting the large pot of pasta off the back burner. She rushed toward the sink and poured the pot into a stainless-steel strainer. "Thank goodness the AC got repaired. Now I know why they're always grilling in the South. Kitchen gets too hot."

"And you're making it hotter," he said, snuggling up to her back, his pelvis fitting against her soft derriere. He scraped back her hair and kissed the damp nape of her neck. She smelled like wildflowers.

His kiss gave her a little shiver. "Keep doing that and we won't make it to dinner."

Cal nibbled his way to the soft slope of her shoulder. "Promise?"

Maggie used a kitchen towel to smack him. "Go sit down and pour yourself a glass of wine. I've spent too much time making this for it to scorch. We've been horny this long. An hour more won't hurt."

He stepped back. "Kinky foreplay? I'm in."

Maggie rolled her eyes and set about chopping up ingredients for what he could only assume was a salad. He'd given her only half an hour in Walmart before they left McKinney and she'd bought enough food for an army. Finding a clean wineglass, he poured some wine and parked himself at the table where he could enjoy the rare sight of a woman making dinner for him. Too often his dates were over hot wings and cold beer at a bar and grill before marathon sex in a sterile hotel room. But it was pleasing to watch Maggie hum as she diced red onion and shredded the block of parmesan. It felt domestic.

He'd rarely given thought to settling down because he'd never felt old enough to want a mortgage or a lawn to mow or kids to splash in a swimming pool. He figured he had too much of his daddy in him. Life on the road suited him.

But he didn't have too many years more to be on the circuit. And he didn't have any backup plans.

Maybe that's what these weird feelings were about. He'd spent years riding bulls, eyeing the prize, but very few thinking about a future beyond the gold buckle. Some of his friends had turned to broadcasting. Others had retired into working as trainers, bull fighters or merely walking off into the sunset never to be heard of again. A handful of former bull riders ran their own ranches. Yet, outside of the one modeling gig, he'd never made a buck that hadn't come from riding the shit out of a pissed-off bull. So what would he do once he hung up his spurs?

He swallowed the doubts.

Jesus, all of this indecisiveness had to be the result of the surgery. He wasn't as young as he used to be and the years of abuse on his body had toughened him. But fatigue had set in, wearing him down. He no longer felt invincible and that had been a left hook to his confidence.

"Here we are," Maggie said, setting the salad on the lazy Susan. He grabbed her and pulled her into his lap for a kiss. She willingly gave it, making his blood sing and his thoughts about-face from the weirdness he'd been experiencing. After several seconds she pried his fingers from her waist and rose. "Soon."

"You like torture, don't you?"

"Don't you find a little buildup more satisfying in the end?"

"No, I find coming satisfying in the end."

Maggie laughed. "Well, there's that."

Five minutes later, she lit two slender candles and switched off the kitchen light. Setting her recently filled wineglass on the table, she finally sat down across from him, where flickering candlelight danced across her soft face. The plate of penne pasta covered with a thick red sauce she'd set in front of him sent up a spicy aroma. Crusty Italian bread sat on either side of the plate, framing her offering. "This is nice, Maggie."

"You're going to need sustenance."

Cal drove his fork into the steaming pasta. "It's been a while since I've gone all night, but I like your confidence in me."

She tucked her napkin in her lap like a lady. "Before we go upstairs and—"

"—get freaky?" he joked, taking a bite. Damn, she knew her way around a kitchen.

"You know I'm not into whips and chains, right?" she asked.

"But you do own thigh-high, black leather boots?"

Maggie made a face. "I hope you don't have great expectations of—"

"Missionary only, huh?"

That made her laugh, but he could see in her demeanor she was nervous. Patience, he reminded himself. Patience. "So tell me about working for Bud."

"You *do* like foreplay," she teased, taking a bite of pasta and nodding at the taste. "Long story short, about two weeks before I was to graduate college, Bud had a stroke that cost him the use of the left side of his body.

It also left him unable to speak well. He asked me to become his personal assistant because he needed someone he trusted to navigate the corporate world for him. Let's just say his family relationships are difficult. Lots of hurt and ugliness from his children. Anyway, I went to work for Bud. Never regretted it."

"But now?"

"After I sell this place, I'm thinking about starting a consulting firm. I'm good at working with people and helping them make good decisions that benefit the company. Somebody somewhere needs someone like me."

I need you.

What an odd thought to pop into his mind. After all, he didn't need anyone like Maggie in his life. His world was exactly what he wanted. As long as he drew a good bull and got a high score at the end of eight seconds, he was gravy. Didn't need anything else.

"Cool," was all he could manage because his thoughts had scared him. He didn't know what was wrong with him. First he'd started doubting his physical ability to compete again in the arena and now an inchworm of dissatisfaction had crawled into his personal life.

Bullshit.

He didn't want to think. He wanted to feel. Specifically, he wanted to feel Maggie shattering in his arms as he drove into her.

This was about sex. Hot, healing, good-for-them-both sex. Nothing more.

So keep that in mind, partner.

Ten minutes later, they slipped onto the porch to finish off the last of the wine. The night was inky and hot, the stars hiding behind clouds that had rolled in. The full moon lurked behind the thin clouds, too, but managed to throw a glow on the land around the sad little porch. Anticipation hadn't faded, but they both seemed to sidestep around it.

Cal didn't want to push to get the sexy started…as if the only reason he'd showered, shaved and showed up had been to get in her pants. That would be too… honest? And it would be a lie. Thing was he liked Maggie. He liked the way she bossed him around, the way she tried to act big city but still blushed when he said something off-color. He liked her laugh and her quick sarcasm. Not to mention, she cooked a damn fine supper. So it felt disingenuous to toss her over his shoulder and run up the stairs to find the nearest bedroom.

"I feel nervous," she said, setting her glass on the rickety rail and rubbing her shoulders as if there was a chill. Which there wasn't.

"Why?"

"I don't know. I mean, I want you, but once we go where we're heading, there's no turning back. We can't undo knowing what each other looks like in our underwear."

"Um, out of our underwear," he said with a laugh, coming up behind her and wrapping his arms around her. He dropped a kiss against her neck. "We don't have to do anything you don't want to do. I want you. God, I want you. But I told you I don't walk into any pasture unless the gate is open."

"I know," she said, falling quiet, but clasping his arms and leaning back into him. He sent a message to the part below his belt to hold off on saluting her body's perfection a few minutes longer.

In the shadows to their left, something moved. His body froze, alarm slamming into him. But then he saw the shape was feline.

"Guess county animal control missed one," Maggie whispered.

He kissed the side of her neck and made her shiver. "Well, one good barn cat is a necessity. It'll keep the rats out of the barn. Snakes, too."

"In that case it can stay." The cat crept into the yard, failing to see them embracing on the porch. Carefully, it made its way toward the barn, belly to the ground.

"So, Maggie," Cal said, squeezing her tight.

"Hmm?"

"Is your gate open or not?"

She stilled for a moment, and then she turned in his arms. Reaching up, she set her hands on his shoulders. Her gaze met his and in her eyes he could see the desire. "Yeah. I took bolt cutters to it."

"In my experience it's the most effective way to get a gate open," he said, lowering his head and capturing her lips with his. She tasted like tangy marinara and wine. Her lips were soft and her body sank into his. Opening her mouth, she gave him exactly what he asked for—full access. After a few seconds, he pulled back and studied her in the faint light.

"Hey," she said, lifting her finger to trace the small scar on his chin. "Thank you."

"For…"

"Being a gentleman."

Cal grinned. "I ain't no gentleman."

"Yeah, you are. You understood what I needed—to decide this for myself. You didn't use my desire against me."

But he'd wanted to. God help him, but if she'd turned him down, he might have resorted to seduction. Wasn't proud of it, but he wanted her so badly. Yet his inclination to give her space had paid off and now he didn't have to step back or press forward. No, he got to hold an armful of sexy, warm woman who tasted like Italian and looked like a swimsuit model. Who said patience didn't pay off?

"I can't say I'm as good as you paint me. In fact, I'm sorta bad. You want to find out how bad I can be?" he asked, trailing a hand down her side, brushing the curve of her breast before grabbing her ass and hauling her against his hardness.

"Ooh," she said, smiling up at him. "I might be interested."

This time she kissed him, going from sweet to hot as hell in a second flat. No longer could he hold back the desire. Her tongue moving against his unleashed all he'd held back.

"Let's go inside. Five weeks starts now," he said.

MAGGIE OPENED THE door to the room she'd been sleeping in for almost a week. The room was small and nothing to brag about, but the bed had a new mattress and clean sheets. And that's all they needed.

She started to turn around and wave her hands with a ta-da motion, but Cal was too quick. He swept her against him, his lips almost punishing. Backing her against the mattress, they fell onto the bed.

"I wanna go slow, but I'm not sure I can. You're all I've been thinking about for a week. Those kick-ass legs, the tight ass and your pretty pair of lips…and every space in between," he said, nipping his way down the column of her throat as he tugged up the hem of her T-shirt.

"If you go slow, I'll kill you." She held his head against her, loving the scratch of his beard on her skin.

She wrapped her legs around his waist, grinding against the hardness that hit exactly where she needed it.

Somehow her T-shirt skimmed her face and went flying behind them, and all the while, Cal never missed a beat in the almost frenzied lovemaking. His hands and mouth were everywhere at once. When he got to the complicated bra clasp, she reached back to unhook the lacy fluff she'd bought on clearance at Barneys last fall. But he obviously had mad skills and the bra popped loose and went sailing overhead before she could help him.

"Oh, sweet…um." He nestled his face between her breasts, inhaling before sucking the left one into his mouth. The sensation made her arch against him. He moved to her other breast, nipping, suckling, making her ache for more.

"Oh, oh," she cried, holding him to her. She wiggled her hips again, rocking against his erection, driving herself toward total loss of control. If there were a launch button, his fingers hovered above it.

Maggie ran her hands up and down his back, tugging at his shirt. Cal paused for a moment and sat back, wrenching his shirt overhead before standing, unbuckling his jeans and allowing them to drop. His boxers joined the orphaned articles of clothing strewn on the floor.

She lifted onto her elbows to take in the splendid sight. Cal was built compactly, all tough sinew and defined muscle. At that very second she got it. All those books with the bare-chested cowboys, all those songs waxing poetic and all those women hanging around the arenas and bars for a shot at one night with a cowboy knew the truth. Cowboys were an addiction. Pure and simple. "Wow."

"No time to admire…or find flaws." He lunged toward her, reaching for the button on the jean shorts she wore. She helped him out, wiggling out of the loose denim, ripping her teeny bikini panties off at the same time so that she was bared to him.

"Holy Moses," Cal breathed, easing onto the bed and running his hand over her stomach down to the thin strip of hair covering the place that ached for him. His finger dipped inside the cleft, grazing her clitoris lightly, making her moan at the sweet pleasure. "Ah, Mags, so wet. So wet for me."

His words turned her to jelly. Legs splayed to either side as she collapsed onto the sheets, uncaring that she looked like a wanton. She couldn't think about the rules of seduction she usually followed—touch here, pet there. Instead she dissolved into a ridiculous mass of nerve endings. Obviously she needed a good screw more than she'd thought she did because the intense pleasure at his touch felt as though she'd achieved nirvana.

For a minute or so she let him have his way because it was too good to stop, but Maggie had never been selfish when it came to the bedroom. Turnabout was fair play. She moved her hand until she clasped the cock bobbing against her thigh. As her fingers curled around his girth, she had but one thought: Cal was the perfect size. The next thought was just as good: he was hard and ready to go.

"Ah," he murmured when she began to move her hand, his body stiffening before relaxing against her. She lifted her gaze to find his eyes squeezed shut, pleasure etched on his face.

The bed creaked as he shifted his weight, lifting so he had better access to her body. His fingers continued the delicious torture, strumming her clit before easing downward, parting her folds. Slowly he slid a finger inside her. And to further torture her, he lowered his head and drew her nipple into the heat of his mouth.

"Oh, please," she said, moving her hips as his fingers established rhythm. Her own fingers did likewise, moving back and forth along the length of his cock.

"What, baby?" he murmured, moving his lips to her other breast.

"I need you now," she said, tugging with just the right amount of force on the erection that filled her hand. "I can't wait. We can do all this later."

All she could think about was him filling her, driving her to the ultimate goal.

Cal pulled himself from her and reached toward the jeans he'd dropped on the floor. Half a second later, he pulled out a string of condoms.

"Ambitious." She laughed, reaching out to stroke the hard ass he half presented her with the action.

"It's one of my most charming qualities," he said with a grin before ripping the package with his teeth. He removed the disk of latex from the package and made quick work of suiting up. Then he leaned down and kissed her, his tongue tangling with hers, a fierce reminder of the frenzy that had swept them earlier.

No more messing around.

Her legs once again fell open as he pressed her back onto the bed. Her knees rose, a welcoming embrace. Cal lifted her hips as he dipped his. And slid home, filling her. "Oh, sweet mother of…" She couldn't finish, because he'd anchored her hips with his big hands and had started moving with hard, long strokes.

Maggie arched her back, lifted her ass and started

moving in time with him. Her hair stuck to her cheeks, her boobs were squished and she'd forgotten to light the candles. Didn't matter because already her body tightened with the release that would come. "I'm close," she panted as he leaned down and bit her nipple.

Inching her hand between them, she found her clit. With his cock hitting her G-spot and her breast sucked into his mouth, all she needed was one little touch. She slammed her other hand down and clenched the sheet as the first wave crashed over her. Her orgasm was intense, making her body tremble and clench.

"Oh. My. Go—" she said before losing her breath again. She'd never come twice, but somehow her body had started and couldn't stop. Vaguely she registered Cal's own guttural groan as he pumped into her, moving her across the bed, but the second orgasm was more intense than the first one.

"Shit," he said, still clasping her hips, emptying himself in her before collapsing.

Maggie's orgasm finally faded, leaving her useless. Hopelessly sated with warm glowing goodness seeping into her bones.

Cal collapsed next to her, his breathing matching hers in raggedness. They both lay looking up at the ceiling, trying to summon words, breaths, something.

Finally, Cal said, "Thank goodness we got the roof fixed. That water stain is scary."

8

MAGGIE LIFTED HERSELF onto her elbows and glanced down at the naked man still panting beside her. "We just had the most amazing sex ever and you're talking about water stains?"

Cal looked like a man who'd been ridden hard and put up wet— a phrase she'd heard one of the painters use. He still wore the spent condom and should have felt vulnerable, maybe even embarrassed. He should not, however, be thinking about work.

"What?" he asked, giving her a slow grin. "You're paying me to fix the water stains. I need to make a note for the painters."

She must have looked disgusted, because he started laughing. Pulling her elbow, he tugged her down. She willingly collapsed again, this time snuggling into his shoulder.

"And I like how you called it 'the best sex ever,'" he teased.

She pinched him on the thigh. "So I like to exaggerate."

He cocked his head. "You mean that wasn't the best

sex ever? Of all time? We didn't set a record for our big, big bang?"

Maggie snorted. "I'm not giving you the satisfaction. You're already too big for your Wranglers."

"That's what she said," he murmured, kissing her temple. "But in all seriousness, Mags, that was at least a nine-point-nine on a scale of one to ten."

"Why wasn't it a ten?" she asked, thinking that after the way she'd achieved multiorgasm she'd have to give it a perfect score. That had never happened before. But then again, she'd never gone almost two years without sex. With another person. Again, Pinkie Lee, her vibrator, didn't count.

"Because we need a goal, babe," he said, giving her a squeeze. "Gotta keep practicing."

She flopped back onto the bed. "That makes sense."

For a few minutes they lay there, comfortable in each other's arms. If Cal was like her, he chased each thought with a new one. Maggie wondered, what was next? Did they settle into something similar to her past relationships? Or would it be hot sex at night and business during the day? They'd set parameters but not particulars. Maybe particulars didn't matter when you were only having a five-week love affair. Or maybe she should stop thinking so much.

Yet planning and overthinking were part of her protection from the riotous world full of mistakes. Potential doom hung over her like a piano dangling from a frayed rope. Though she'd convinced herself she didn't mind the mistake her mother had made in getting knocked up by some unknown man and not caring to find him afterward, it still molded her beliefs about relationships. She didn't lie when she said she had had a good childhood, but that didn't mean she wanted the same for her future children. If she even decided to have children. Decisions mattered. Newton had pretty much nailed that with the whole "for each action there's an equal and opposite reaction" thing. No decision stood without repercussion. Without ripples.

So what would be her ripple with Cal?

"You hungry?" Cal asked, rising and snapping off the condom. He padded naked out the door and a second later she heard the water in the bathroom turn on.

"Why are men always hungry after sex?" she called to him.

The water shut off and three seconds later his head popped past the doorjamb. "Because I did all the work."

"Well, next time, I'll do the work." She reached over and flipped on the bedside lamp, illuminating the room.

His blue eyes darkened and like a snap of her fingers, desire came roaring back. "I'll take you up on that. I'll even give you pointers for the ride."

"I don't need pointers." She scrambled up, tucking her feet beneath her. Her breasts swayed and Cal's eyes went immediately to the jiggle. Her friends in college had always teased her about the boob job she'd gotten in high school. She hadn't gotten one, of course. Mother Nature had been her plastic surgeon. A boon since Cal was obviously a breast man.

"Your tits are magnificent," he said, moving back into the room. His cock lengthened and thickened, making her heart beat hard.

"These little ol' things?" she asked cupping them and glancing down.

"You know what you're doing," he said, setting one knee on the bed, crossing his arms. He looked rather magnificent posed that way. His biceps looked bigger, his chest wider and his stomach somehow trimmer. And there was that erection rising to the occasion.

"Who, me?" she said, dropping her hands and swinging her legs to the other side, very deliberately doing them one at a time à la *Basic Instinct*.

Cal threw his head back and laughed. "You're a minx."

She grinned. "A cowboy who uses the term *minx*?"

"What? We're all spittin', cussin' dumb asses? I went to college, you know. Even took some classes."

"Which taught you the word *minx*?"

"I took Cary Grant 101," Cal said, lowering himself so that his hands sank into the bed. He looked like a predator stalking her. Somehow it fueled her blood. She wanted him to catch her and do bad things to her.

"Did you smoke cigarettes, sip Scotch and practice tying bowties?" She laughed, putting her hands down and leaning forward so they were nose to nose. Her breasts swung toward him and he looked down.

"How'd you know?" he asked, kissing her.

"Lucky guess," she said, kissing him back. "You ready for round two or you want to cut into that lemon pie I picked up?"

"Both?" He wiggled his eyebrows as he lifted a hand to cup her breast.

Like a button pushed, her eyes closed and her nipples tightened. The achy throb in her pelvis returned. "Sounds kinky."

Giving her breast a squeeze, he said, "I'm now having whipped cream fantasies. I'll be right back." He climbed off the bed, slipping on his boxers before he hurried out the door.

Maggie collapsed onto the bed with a laugh. The man

wanted to rub whipped cream and lemon filling on her and lick it off. Sounded messy. And sticky. She'd probably have to wash the sheets. "Don't forget to bring some forks."

"We won't need forks," he called back.

CAL GRABBED THE pie from the fridge and pried off the plastic lid. He'd never combined food and sex. Except one time in Cheyenne when a chick went down on him while he was eating his burger in the parking lot of Big Barn Burgers. He'd nearly choked on the damn thing.

He stared down at the pie covered with fancy loops of whipped cream. They always did things like this in the movies. Whip cream bikinis or pouring honey over a woman's breasts were, like, sensual things. Couldn't be weird. After all, he loved lemon pie. And Maggie's body. Combining the two would be amazing.

Or strange.

He shrugged, grabbed two forks just in case he changed his mind, and jogged up the stairs, very aware of his heavy cock slapping against his upper thigh. He couldn't believe he already wanted her again. He felt like a teenager. Not to mention he'd noticed only a slight twinge in his shoulder as he made love to her. Had to be a good sign.

When he entered the room, he found Maggie propped up against the headboard. She'd stacked pillows behind her back. She lounged against the white sheets, one leg crossed over her bent knee, bobbing in time to the music coming out of her phone. Bruno Mars. "You look amazingly sexy."

She smiled. "I'm showing my good side."

"It's a very nice side," he said, setting the pie on the

bedside table and sliding a hand down to the ass revealed in her pose.

Maggie eyed the pie. "I see you brought forks. So
you're chickening out on food play?"

"Is that what it's called? Hell, you're the city girl. I
just call this a snack."

She laughed and he decided she needed to do that
more. It wasn't that she was serious all the time. Maggie
had plenty of sass. But something shadowed her. Perhaps it was the same thing that followed him—a need
to prove himself. To rise from a hard beginning, a life
stacked against them, to sit in the sunshine and enjoy the
reward. He'd done much to make that happen. Another
world championship would sweeten the pot.

"A snack, huh?" she said, swiping a finger through
the whipped cream.

"Hey, you're messing it up," he teased.

She held her finger to his lips. He sucked the cream
from her finger.

"Never mind. Mess it up," he said with a grin. Maggie
dipped her finger back into the cream and then popped
it into her mouth.

"Yum," she said, closing her eyes. "Hand me a fork…
and take off your boxers."

"You're not going to rub that on me, are you?" he
asked, shimmying out of his boxers and kicking them
to the side. He climbed back onto the bed.

"No, I don't want to be the only one who's naked,"
she said, lifting the pie from the side table and grabbing
a fork. "Let's dig in. Then make love."

He settled in next to her, crossing his feet at the ankles
and took a bite of the pie. It was decent. Nothing like
the one his mom picked up in Dallas, but he'd rather eat

a subpar pie with Maggie naked than a prize-winning one listening to Gary complain about the grass growing in the wrong direction. "So obviously, I intended on making this a sexy little adventure, but I figured we didn't want to change the sheets tonight. Does that make me boring?"

Maggie laughed. "Is it okay I had the same thought? Though showering with you might be fun."

"Oh, we'll get to that," he said, reaching out to wipe a smear of pie from the corner of her mouth. He sucked his thumb into his mouth. "So where will you start your company, Mags?"

"You don't want to…oh, do you need a bit more time?" Maggie took another bite of the pie, shooting an uncertain look at him.

"No," he said, slightly offended she would suggest such a thing. "I wanted to know a little more about you. Unless you want to—"

"No, I mean, yes, but it's okay to talk, too." Maggie dug her fork into the pie. "You know, I don't have a firm plan for my business in mind. I suppose I will either stay in Philly or move to New Jersey which would be close to NYC."

"New Jersey, huh?" Sounded horrible. But then again, he'd only visited the state a few times.

Maggie shrugged. "It makes sense. My mother now lives there with my aunt, so I would have family close. I think it's the right move. Helping stubborn board members see the other person's view was something I was actually good at. Probably because I spent my early years watching my mother negotiate everything with Bud's wife. Phyllis was an absolute bitch. Don't know why Bud married her."

"Probably money. Or knowing her family. Rich people still do stuff like that."

"Yeah, she came from money and was probably a lot nicer before she had three spoiled brats and a botched nose job. An ugly nose makes people cranky," Maggie said, licking her spoon thoughtfully. The move reminded him they were both splendidly naked in bed. "All I need is the cash to get it started. If I can sell the Triple J for enough money, I can cobble a business plan together."

"Interesting," he said, wondering why anyone would want to serve as a negotiator, putting up with stubborn businessmen. And people thought he was crazy for riding bulls. At least he didn't have to listen to bulls.

"Not really, but I have to find something to pay the bills. As of now, I no longer have a place to live or a job. My aunt's place in Newark is a two-bedroom walk-up. So…yeah."

He scraped the graham crust bottom and popped it in his mouth. "Okay, enough talk. We were supposed to be rubbing whipped cream on each other and licking it off."

Maggie scooped up some pie and allowed it to drop on his stomach. "Oops."

His stomach contracted because it was cold.

"Guess I better clean that up," Maggie said, swinging the hacked up pie over to the bedside table. She leaned over and licked the lemon filling and cream off his stomach.

Yeah, it was sticky and messy and…frickin' hot.

Because she didn't stop. She rolled over, presenting a nice ass for his contemplation, and took several long licks before lifting her gaze to his. "Was this what you were thinking?"

He swallowed. "Um, pretty much."

"Or maybe this?" she asked, reaching over him and scooping up more cream. This time she smeared it lower than his stomach. Her fingers were light as they dragged across his cock which grew hard at her touch even though the cream was cold. But the cold didn't last long because Maggie's warm mouth enveloped him. She sucked all the dessert off, leaned back and grinned. "This is the best pie I've ever eaten."

Cal gave a choking laugh. Because he hadn't expected her to do something so spontaneous.

He sprang toward her, catching her arms, knocking her back onto the bed, making her squeal. "Speaking of eating pie."

She started wriggling when he reached out and grabbed the pie tin. "Don't you dare put that on me."

He slathered a fair dollop across her breasts. Something about the oily whipped cream and those firm, rounded mounds worked. He smoothed the cream over them, lazily swiping his fingers through, lifting them to suck the sweetness off. Maggie had stopped laughing and lay there watching him. He could see she was definitely turned on.

"What a mess," he said with a gleam in his eyes.

"You should clean up after yourself," she said.

"Don't mind if I do," he said, bending and sucking one of her nipples into his mouth. She made a strangled noise and squirmed against the sheets. He didn't stop. Instead he turned his attention to the other breast, laving the whipped cream off, making little *mmm* sounds. She tasted delicious without the whipped cream so he didn't stop, though the white fluff was nowhere to be found.

"Please," Maggie moaned, tugging his head.

"I'm not finished," he said, reaching over to the pie and dropping another scoop onto her belly.

"Oh," she said, as he went to work licking the cream off her flat belly. He dipped his tongue into her navel, making his way down to her pubic bone. Cleaning up his mess in a most wicked way, leaving her sticky and, judging by the way her hips kept bucking, very horny.

"There," he said, dusting his hands. "All clean."

Maggie cracked an eye at him. "You're done?"

"Unless there's something else that needs attending to."

She grabbed a pillow and hit him with it.

"What?" he yelped, tackling her and rolling her onto his body. She was definitely sticky…and wet. He felt the slickness of her slide against his thigh.

"You big tease," she said, kissing him, biting his lower lip.

"Says the pot to the kettle," he said, grabbing her ass and moving her so her mound ground against his cock. Felt like heaven and must have been good for her, too, because she closed her eyes and sighed. Cal lifted his torso from the bed, taking her with him.

"What are you doing?" she asked, sliding off him. He tossed a few pillows toward the headboard before picking her up and setting her against their fluffy down.

Giving her a quick kiss, he tugged her hips forward a little. "I'm cleaning up my mess."

"What?"

He took her hands and set them on her knees. And then he pushed her knees up so that she was open to him. "You're a little messy down there. Hold your legs back."

Her face grew red and she started to drop her legs. "This is sorta…uh…"

"No," he said, stopping her, pushing her knees back again. "You're so beautiful, so freaking hot. I want to taste you. I want you for dessert."

Pushing her knees farther apart, he dragged his gaze from the most appealing of sights to her smoky topaz eyes. "Hold your knees, darlin'."

Then he bent and parted her folds, moaning in satisfaction at how wet she was. Her flesh was pink and perfect, the bud of her clitoris shielded by a tiny hood. Carefully he pulled back her plump lips and dragged his tongue through her heat. She tasted much like that lemon pie, slightly tart, mostly sweet. And she smelled of their earlier sex—an aphrodisiac. He feared he'd come right there on the sheets.

He took his time playing with her. Going slow, sliding his fingers inside her tightness, flicking her clit with his tongue. He'd work her, and then he'd let up, content to kiss her soft thighs. The wiggle of her ass and her sighs and groans told him all he needed to know. She was close, but he wanted it to last. So he gave and he took.

"Please, please," she begged, thrusting herself toward his mouth.

"Ah, I love you like this, Mags. Out of control," he said, sliding two of his fingers inside her, hooking them so he found the spot that would help take her over the edge. Then he fastened his mouth on her clit and sucked gently.

She came hard and fast, shaking as her fingers slipped and her legs closed around his head. She screamed as another orgasm tore through her.

Cal never let up. He held her hips, enjoying the warm gush, the slurping sounds he made as he took her again and again to climax.

"You have to stop," she said, pulling at his ears. "I can't… It's enough."

Cal lifted himself, grabbed the condoms he'd set on the table by the pie, and ripped open a package. "It's never enough."

Maggie looked spent. He pulled her ass toward him and her legs stayed splayed. He looked down at her, rosy and flushed. Large breasts heaving, thighs open to reveal her treasure. He'd never seen anyone hotter than this women. She made him hard as a fence post.

He lifted her ass and slid home. She was tight and hot and wet and everything a woman should be.

"Oh." She stiffened, arching her back.

"That's a girl," he murmured, kissing her neck. "Let's come again, baby. This time together."

And then he started moving, pulling her hips to him as he thrust deep.

"Oh, no…oh, no…oh, no," Maggie chanted in his ear. "I can't…this is…ahhh."

Her body tightened, gripping his cock as she came again. The pulsating pressure tipped him over the edge. His balls tightened, that sweet pain gathering deep in his pelvis and…then blessed release.

"Oh, shit," he said, anchoring her hips, spilling himself inside her. Jolts of pleasure vibrated through his body, making chill bumps cover his thighs and arms. He gave one last jerk and collapsed on top of her.

And found she was coming again.

That made him laugh.

She was like an engine. Once you pulled the string, she purred to life and didn't stop. He'd revved her into a new dimension. Her breath came hard as if she'd run a race. Maybe it was like a race. It had been one helluva sex marathon, that was for sure.

"Oh, my dear Bessie," Maggie said after she stopped pulsating. "That was incredible."

He could only nod, then flop off her. All energy had fled, leaving him absolutely bushed. He wasn't even certain he could lift his head and deal with postcoital cleanup. So he lay there, staring up at the shadows etched on the ceiling, enjoying the feel of her next to him. Usually after having sex, he liked to get up, pull on his boots and get going. But for some unexplained reason, he wanted to stay with her. Sleep in this bed. Watch the light of dawn caress her cheeks. Be there when her pretty eyes opened.

Maybe it was because she wasn't some one-night stand. He'd see her over the next few weeks every single day. Why not relax and wake up next to a pretty woman without the stale taste of tequila in his mouth paired with the guilt of knowing he'd never call?

"You know," Maggie said, her breath finally evening. "That *is* a pretty nasty water stain."

Cal laughed. "I'll add primer to the list."

9

THE CAT SHE'D seen a few days ago was a female and if Maggie was any judge of animals, she'd say Kitty Girl was preggers.

"Here, girl," Maggie said, holding out a piece of chicken. The cat sat in the shadow of the barn, blinking at her as if it couldn't be bothered. Every few seconds, the cat let out a plaintive meow. Such a tease. "Come on. I won't touch you. It's really good."

The cat turned her head away.

"You still working on that cat?" Charlie asked as he walked by, carrying two pails of something that sloshed over the sides.

Maggie didn't answer. Merely looked up at him because it should be fairly clear she was trying to get the cat to trust her.

"She's feral and don't trust you. Gotta give her time," he said, not looking bothered in the least that she didn't respond.

Thank you, King of Obvious. "She's pregnant and needs veterinary care."

"Pshaw," Charlie said, spitting in the hot Texas dirt.

"She don't need no vet. Kittens will come out fine the way they're intended to. Happens all the time."

"But there could be complications," Maggie insisted, knowing Charlie thought she was an idiot, but not caring. She'd seen plenty of shows on Animal Planet where kittens got stuck during the birthing process.

"Ah, leave her alone and she'll be fine. You can pick a kitten out of the litter if you want. Maybe one that will cuddle with you because that cat ain't." The man sounded disgusted and started moving away from her. He smelled like whiskey, but he'd showed up each day and put in a good day's work. There was still a strange vibe between him and Cal, but when she mentioned it, Cal clammed up or changed the subject.

"Hey, Charlie," she called, tossing the meat toward the cat and rising. The older man stopped in his tracks and turned, lifting an eyebrow.

She swiped at the sweat threatening to roll into her eyes. Mid-July in Texas was hotter than the devil's ass crack. Another term she'd heard from the painters. They were full of gems.

"Huh?" he asked.

"What's going on between you and Cal?"

The older man flinched. In that reaction, she could see that she hadn't imagined the coldness. "How should I know? Besides what business is it of yours anyhow?"

"It's not. He doesn't say anything about it, but it's obvious you two don't care for each other."

Charlie turned. "No need to. Whatever we had is water under the bridge."

"So you *do* have something between you," she said, crossing her arms.

The older man didn't answer. Merely moved off away from her prying questions.

Maggie brushed her hands against her shorts and started back toward the house, not knowing why she'd bothered to ask. Maybe it was because Cal was such a closed book. Sure, he flirted, told stories about towns he'd visited and took her breath away every night, but he didn't talk about anything of substance. If she brought up Charlie or his injury or even his future after bull riding, Cal went silent.

Wanting to understand a man better wasn't a crime, was it? She knew they'd drawn boundaries, but something seemed to burden Cal. She suspected his shoulder wasn't getting better and that worried him. She saw the wincing, the way he rubbed it subconsciously. But there was something more. Like a sore beneath the saddle. She wasn't sure if it had to do with Charlie, his family, his doubts or the whole of Coyote Creek.

But it shouldn't matter to her. They were what they were. And what they were was down to four more weeks.

Then they'd be a memory.

Maggie sighed and opened the screened door to the kitchen. She'd spent all morning painting the lower bedrooms while Cal pulled up the flooring in the kitchen. A crew would come in to lay down the new tile she'd selected from a local flooring place Cal had recommended. He'd suggested the more local she could buy, the better. Invited goodwill and talk that might lead to a potential buyer for the Triple J.

Maggie hadn't listed the ranch yet. She wanted to complete the renovation before she got tangled up in a real estate contract. She'd love to be able to sell the place herself, but since she'd likely have to leave Texas with the place still on the market and didn't have any experience with ranching, she figured the Realtor's fee would be worth the money she'd probably lose in doing her own negotiations.

Cal stood in the middle of the kitchen, shirtless, holding a metal bar and cussing.

"What's wrong?"

"Whoever put this son of a bitch in last time must have made a bargain with the devil. This shit won't come up." He threw the bar down. And then winced and grabbed his shoulder. "This isn't working."

Maggie opened the fridge and pulled out a beer. Man pacifier. "Here."

He took the beer and popped the top, grunting his thanks.

"I know you wanted to work and give your shoulder some natural motions rather than doing merely therapy exercises, but this is too much for one man."

"The hell it is." He lifted the beer and chugged it. Sweat coated his body like some kind of fantasy. If only he weren't so frustrated…and there weren't so many workers surrounding them. She'd had the best sex of her life over the past week. They'd had sex in the shower, on the freshly waxed stairs and once in the rocking chair out front. That particular feat had been almost dangerous because there were so many rotten boards. She'd made plenty of sweet memories in the stillness of the hot Texas nights.

But Cal seemed itchy today.

"What's up with you?" she asked, grabbing a beer for herself.

"Nothing."

She leveled a look at him.

"I'm frustrated today, is all. Damn floors are a bitch to get up and my shoulder's hurting. Bucking barrel came in and I haven't had time to even set it up."

"Let's do it now," Maggie said.

"Naw, it's okay. I have time. I'll do it later." He set the bottle on the counter and turned from her. They'd had a week of laughter, good sex and companionship. Right now, all of that was absent. Maggie understood. A person could only sustain happy for so long. Real life didn't allow for total bliss 24/7.

Reality had sharp teeth that nipped at happy.

"You sure? I don't mind. In fact, I can't wait for you to show me how to ride," she said, lobbing sexual innuendo into his court.

Cal's eyes shuttered. "Nah. I'll do it later."

He didn't hit it back. And at that moment, she understood why. Her strong, fearless bull rider was afraid.

Hard to accept a man full of smiles and rock-hard confidence, among other rock-hard things, could be afraid of anything. But there it was in the tight lines around his mouth and in the flicker of something in the depths of his blue eyes. Cal was afraid to climb on the bucking barrel.

But why?

He was a two-time world champion. She'd gone to the PBR website and watched him ride several bulls. *Phenomenal* wasn't even the word for the man. He was grace and grit atop the bulls, his body nearly fluid as he rode the twisting, turning creatures. She'd held her breath watching him, fingers pressed to her lips. She'd never seen anything that made her want to cheer, scream and hide her eyes more than Cal clinging to the back of a bull.

She took another draw on the Texas-made beer. "You said you'd give me pointers."

"That was on riding me," he said, his face relaxing.

"I'm already good at that, but practice makes perfect."

He took another gulp of beer. "I guess we can set it up tonight."

"Good."

"Will you do it topless?" he asked, his lips twitching as he turned back into the teasing Cal she knew.

"Is that a dare? Or a suggestion?" she asked, grabbing the brushes from the sink and setting them in the roller bin splattered with paint.

"Whichever one will make you do it. Because your—"

"I know. You have a great fascination with the girls. I'm almost jealous of my boobs."

"You should be. If I could live between your tits, I would."

"But it would make bull riding awfully awkward. Try explaining why I have to sit in front of you when you ride."

Cal laughed. Mission accomplished. Grumpy Cal had climbed into the backseat so the wicked, sexy cowboy could drive. She slid by him, dropping a kiss on his mouth. He tasted like sweat and beer. Which meant a second longer kiss.

Then Maggie climbed the stairs to fetch the rollers and drop cloths. Last night they'd slept in Cal's trailer in order to escape the fumes. The carpets had been ripped up to reveal pretty wood floors. Cal had suggested they refinish them themselves, but Maggie knew her limits. So he'd found a husband and wife team that would come next week and sand and refinish the oak planks. They'd look good with pretty hooked rugs and old iron bedsteads on them, but Maggie wouldn't get the chance to see pretty sheer curtains at the newly paned windows or an antique rocking chair sitting in the corner. The rooms would be a blank canvas for the new owners.

The hours flew by as she rocked out to Lenny Kravitz and chilled to James Taylor. The walls dried to a perfect shade and the room took on a bright, fresh hue. When Cal tapped her on the shoulder, she screeched, pulling the earbuds out. "Jesus, you scared the pants off me."

"I wish," he joked, eyeing the short shorts now streaked with light gray paint. Then he lifted his gaze, turning a circle. "I like this color. This place is going to look like a totally new house."

"I know," she said, trying to keep the wistful tone from her voice. Not that she was getting attached, but it was the first place she'd ever owned. For at least another month, nearly four hundred acres belonged to her, not to mention 3,215 square feet of ranch house. The thought satisfied her for some reason. "How are things coming with the floor?"

"I called for help," he said, handing her an ice water.

"A man who actually listens to a woman's suggestion? I may have to sell tickets to this experience."

Cal made a face. "I'm not that stubborn. Well, I am, but I finally realized I can't do the floors alone."

"And you admit you're not invincible? I'm waiting for lightning to strike."

"Very funny," he said, catching her around her waist. "Has anyone ever told you how sexy you look streaked with paint?"

"Actually, yes."

Cal frowned. "Who was he? Where does he live? And do you have any spare ammunition lying around?"

"It would be hard to find the entire fraternity at La Salle University. I helped paint their chapter room one summer. Lots of suggestions regarding helping me clean the paint off."

Cal kissed her. "I hate them all."

She raised on her toes and kissed him again, allowing her breasts to brush his still bared chest. He smelled like sweat and hot man. Addictive. "Did the others leave already?"

"Yeah, Charlie said the guys rebuilding the porch had to go for more decking nails. They'll be back tomorrow morning with those infernal nail guns." He gave an exaggerated glower.

"Let's call it quits and go pick up your barrel thing. My arms ache from all the painting, anyway." She brushed her pelvis against the hardening cock in his jeans. "But I may need some help getting this paint off first."

Cal slid his hand into her shorts, caressing her ass cheek. "I'm willing to scrub wherever you need me to scrub." His fingers slid toward the wetness gathering between her thighs. She raised up on her tiptoes and parted her legs so he could have access.

"Good," she said, rocking her pelvis so her cleft rubbed his hardness. A jolt of pleasure slammed into her. "After we, uh, shower, we can go into town. I need boots."

"It's hot to be wearing boots," he said, though he wore them. He dropped his head and nibbled her sweaty neck. The feel of him sucking her flesh lightly and rubbing his hands over the globe of her ass caused heat to sink into her pelvis. She felt herself grow wetter.

"Flip-flops aren't much protection against snakes and

random nails. Plus, it would be nice to have a souvenir of Texas," she managed to say.

Cal unbuttoned her shorts and pushed them down her hips, leaving her clad in a tiny bikini. Then he dropped to his knees and pressed a kiss to her belly before nuzzling her satin-covered mound with his nose. Looking up he said, "We can go to the Co-op. I need cement for the bucking barrel, anyway. If we get moving, I'll have enough time to stop by Whitman's Hardware before they close."

Maggie sighed as his hands cupped her ass and brought her hard against his mouth. "But we have to shower first."

"Don't worry. We'll take a fast one together. Conserve water," he said, fastening his mouth on the satin that covered her clitoris. He stroked her with his tongue through the material.

Maggie knew what he was doing. Driving her to distraction. "I know what will happen when we get naked and soaped up in that shower."

Cal released her ass, held up his hands and looked up at her. "Hey, I can keep my hands to myself."

"But not your mouth," she said, tangling her hand through his hair and pressing him back to his previous task.

He obliged, nuzzling her flesh through the now-soaked panties. Maggie sighed and dropped her head back, letting him do as he pleased. He sucked and nibbled before sliding the material aside. She felt the heat of his breath on her naked flesh as she felt the pressure grow in her womb. Cal made one long slow swipe of his tongue through her sex. Then he stood. "Last one in the shower has to do the dishes tonight."

Maggie blinked at the sudden loss of pleasure. Cal grinned as he darted out of the room.

"You bastard, you know I hate doing the dishes," she shouted with a laugh. But truly she didn't, not with Cal sitting at the kitchen table strumming songs on his old guitar. There was something comforting about his baritone while she scrubbed the pots.

Yeah, this place was growing on her.

And that determined cowboy was growing on her, too.

That thought was more dangerous than the snake she saw coiled in the road. Way more dangerous. Buying cowboy boots wasn't going to protect her from either of them.

10

Cal scanned the rack of boots. "We can always drive back into McKinney. Go to Cavender's."

"And get mugged by your fans? No thanks," Maggie said, holding up a brown leather Justin roper and squinting at it.

"I ain't that popular, darlin'." He tried for lazy charm in his demeanor since he'd lost his cool earlier. But he hadn't liked letting her see how frustrated he was by his damn inability to control his body. Ripping up the floor had hurt his shoulder like a mother. It pissed him off. That and the fact he'd had words with his mother about Wyatt on Sunday. It had started with his brother, Wyatt, asking questions about riding bulls. They'd finished lunch and sat in the sunroom drinking sweet tea. Wyatt had grabbed a rope and practiced tying it.

"So you still thinking about riding, huh?" Cal said to Wyatt, eyeing the rope in his brother's hand. The kid looked like Gary Whitehorse's Comanche ancestors with the exception of his brown eyes and gangly build. Seventeen and ready to conquer, Wyatt was buck wild and spoiled rotten by his father. The kid's saving grace was he had a good heart and a mother who'd beat him before she'd let him come to a bad end.

A mulish expression crossed the kid's face. Cal knew that look. Seen it too often in the mirror. "Yeah. Why not?"

"You're too tall."

"Whatever. I'm just messing around, anyway."

"Just messing around can get your face broken," Cal said, noting his mother's back stiffening. Ruth had lost Cal to the sport. She wouldn't lose Wyatt.

Cal didn't know whether he should support his younger brother's dream of bull riding or squash it before the kid tore himself apart. On one hand it gave them something in common. Cal had been on the road during much of Wyatt's boyhood, driving incredible distances until he hit the PBR and started making enough to fly to the venues. And there had been no breaks. He rode all year, chasing the rankings, battling through broken noses, gashes and strained muscles. No time for Coyote Creek. But despite the fire in the kid's eyes, Cal had seen enough to know his kid brother would never achieve success as a bull rider.

"I ain't afraid if that's what you're implying," Wyatt said, brown eyes flashing with anger.

"Did I say that?" Cal asked.

Wyatt made good grades and as he approached his senior year of high school, he had a good shot of getting an academic scholarship. But Cal figured he'd have to toss Wyatt a bone, and in the process of letting him try bull riding, he might knock some sense into the kid.

For a few seconds the kid stared down at the rope. "One of the guys over at the Co-op said you ordered a bucking barrel in. Maybe I can come out and try it."

Cal nodded. "I could use some help getting it installed. You can shovel."

"I can do that," Wyatt said.

Ruth caught Cal's eye and she glared at him. Battle lines drawn. "Can I speak to you for a minute, Cal?"

Wyatt rolled his eyes as Cal and their mother rose. The kid knew what their mother wanted. Same song, different dance.

"You have to nip this in the bud," his mother whispered, spinning on him, her finger jabbing him in the chest.

"Mom, I've got this," Cal said, taking her finger out of his solar plexus.

"No, you don't. That's all he does is watch you and all your friends ride. He's glued to his laptop, streaming all your rodeos."

"And you're not?" He still wanted his mom to watch, to be proud of him. To not hate the sport he loved so much. But she had issues with rodeo. The sport had brought Cal's father to town...and it had taken him away.

"Of course. And I live with my heart in my throat, scared to death. And when Rasputin tossed you, gored you and stomped on you, I felt like it was happening to me."

"Mom," Cal began.

"No. You don't understand. I'm proud of you. I am. But I can't go through it again. You and I both know that Wyatt isn't cut out for it. He's too tall and he's starting too late. He'll get hurt."

"But you have to let me handle it. If you push him away, he'll only hold on tighter. Let me spend some time with him. He can come out to the ranch and I'll put him to work. He can earn a little cash and I'll teach him to ride. After a few weeks, I'll take him over to Sawyer's and get him on a practice bull. Hal Sawyer will tell him straight up that he won't cut the mustard. Better he hear it from someone in the business than me or you."

Ruth made a face. "But he could still get hurt."

"Nah, maybe a bump or bruise. Maybe enough to give 'em up for good."

"Like you did?" his mother said wryly.

Cal smiled. "Well, if he gets addicted, I can't do much about it. He's fascinated enough to want a ride, but I'm not sure the passion and work ethic are there yet."

"But the sense of adventure and all those girls are. It's such a lure. Look at the life you lead."

He knew she was thinking, "like father, like son." Cal's father had lived the same vagabond lifestyle. Handsome as sin and just as shiftless, he'd rolled into town thirty-six years ago and hired on to help with branding, saving money for his next ride. Ruth had been a teenage waitress with plans to leave the five-stoplight town for a chance at modeling in LA. But she'd taken one look at Dave Calhoun's baby blues and that had been all she wrote. Ten months later she had a newborn, a used trailer and an empty spot in her bed. Dave hadn't stuck around long enough to learn to change a diaper before he was gone again. She'd tracked him down in Wyoming. A woman had come to the pay phone and told her Dave was with her now and to stop pestering him. Ruth never looked for Cal's father again.

So she probably thought Cal was like his old man, roaming around, a new girl in each town. The thing was Cal wondered the same thing. Maybe he understood his old man better than he thought…though Cal would have never knocked a woman up and then abandoned her and their child. Never. But that itch to move, that empty feeling in his belly, seemed never fulfilled.

Maggie pulled him from his recollections with a sigh. "How do you do it?"

"Do what?" he asked, bending down to peer at the lower shelf lined with boots. A pair of sand-colored boots caught his eyes. Weren't Lucchese, but they sported nice leather tooling and looked comfortable enough.

"Sound like such a cowboy. It's so hot."

"That's just how we talk down here. Ain't like I'm using it for effect or nothing. Here, try these, baby." He shoved the boots toward her.

"Oh, these are pretty."

He liked the way her eyes lit up. "Then they'll definitely suit you."

"You don't have to say things like that to get me into bed," she teased.

"I know. 'Cause once you've been with Cal Lincoln, you're ruined for other men," he said, pulling her hip toward him, rubbing a hand on her bared shoulder.

Maggie's hair tumbled around her shoulders and her cheeks looked rosy. Like a well-loved woman's should. Her skin had grown tan from all the work she'd done washing windows, pulling weeds and tilling flower beds. Even though she'd worked like a dog—something that had surprised the hell out of him—she looked healthy and relaxed. She hadn't lied when she implied she'd needed sex. He'd patched her up real good and he'd send her back to Philly ready to…

Something terrible bloomed inside his head.

It was the image of a faceless man gripping Maggie's hips, nibbling his way down her collarbone. Then he saw her throw her head back as the stranger tugged the band from her ponytail, making sweet waves of brown silk tumble over her naked shoulders. Her breasts heaved as the man licked first one nipple, then the other.

Furious jealousy seized him, sinking its claws into him, shaking him.

His hands curled so he jabbed them into the front pocket of his jeans and turned away. He didn't want to feel this way about her. He'd told her they were about five weeks of pleasure. Thinking about her with another man shouldn't make him incensed…ready to punch his fist through something. But despite his best effort to keep his distance, he did, indeed, care about Maggie. Thing was, the woman delighted him. From cooking him dinner to refusing help with the tiller to her willingness to tangle with a perceived threat to her status as his woman, everything she did charmed him. He loved too much about her. Even those ridiculous house shoes with the floppy bunny ears she'd worn the past few mornings.

"I talked to Charlie today," she said, sitting on the bench and sliding off the flip-flop she wore.

"Why?" he said drolly.

"I wanted to know why you two act so weird around each other," she said.

Cal's jealousy faded and irritation took its place. Just when he thought everything about her was perfect, she started meddling. "Nothing like coming out of the corner with a sucker punch."

Maggie looked up at him, her forehead crinkled as she struggled to pull the boot on. "Surprise attack worked for the Pict peoples who occupied ancient Scotland. It was one of the main reasons they built Hadrian's Wall. Very effective."

"History lesson aside, why do you care about me and Charlie?" Cal asked.

"I don't know. You go out of your way to avoid him and I wondered," she said, obviously refusing to drop the subject.

Did the Picts know when to retreat? 'Cause now would be a good time for Maggie to do that. "If you're implying I'm emotionally crippled, that's horseshit."

"I merely wondered why you both circle each other like snarling yard dogs."

She definitely wasn't going to drop it. "We have history. Nothing worth repeating."

"That's what he said."

"Did he?" Cal wouldn't have expected Charlie to open up to Maggie, but then again, the old man seemed to have a soft spot for women and children. That was likely his only redeeming quality. "Okay, fine. Charlie taught me to ride bulls. He actually taught me a lot of things— roping, branding, sittin' a horse in a rainstorm."

Her head jerked up as if she hadn't actually expected him to tell her. "He's the person who taught you to ride a bull?"

"Yeah, before he went to work as a ranch hand, he rodeoed. I was a little wild and he hired me to work one summer. We clicked. Charlie taught me the cowboy code."

"Cowboy code?"

"Things like a man always takes care of his horse before himself, how to tie knots, shoot a pistol. Just things a guy needs to know if he works in the saddle."

"But you don't work in a saddle."

"I did for a while. I've worked a spread or two in my lifetime," Cal said, finding another pair of boots that looked nice and holding them up to her. She shook her head. "We had a falling-out when I was eighteen."

"Oh." She stilled and waited for him to continue.

Hell, she was like every other woman. She wanted to fix things, make everyone hunky-dory, latching arms and singing "Kumbaya." He'd have to spill or he'd look emotionally damaged or like he was at fault. He wasn't. Charlie was the one who'd lost his marbles.

"It started with my mom going out with Charlie when I was in high school. Long story short, he fell for her. She didn't fall for him. When I was a senior, she started dating Gary, who she's now married to. Charlie convinced me to interfere on his behalf. It caused some drama. She married Gary, anyway, and Charlie took to the bottle. He got mean."

"You stopped training with him?"

"Not at that point. See, I got a scholarship to University of Texas to play baseball. Everyone thought it was a no-brainer that I go to UT, but I wanted to be a bull rider so I told the MLB team that drafted me along with UT that I wasn't going to play baseball. It pissed my mother off."

"Wow. You turned down a baseball scholarship to ride bulls? That takes a lot of self-assurance. And passion for rodeo."

"Two things I have in buckets," he said, finally finding a smile. He'd known since his first ride he was destined to be a bull rider.

"So what happened?" she asked.

"I got thrown my freshman year of college. Ended up with a bad concussion. Charlie came to Southeast Oklahoma State where I was on partial scholarship. My mom came, too. She'd just given birth to Wyatt and she was hopped up on hormones. It wasn't a good scene. She cried, Charlie yelled at my advisor for putting me in danger and Mom yelled at Charlie for interfering. It was a real crap storm."

Her gaze was riveted to him.

"Charlie had always been a quiet, reasonable man, but I guess the booze did something to him. He threatened my mother, my coach and half the rodeo team."

"With a gun?"

"No, but they called the police on him.

"To make matters worse, the doctor told my mother I had possible brain damage so she threatened to sue the college. That paired with Charlie's crazy altercation got me dropped from the rodeo team. Then Gary called the MLB scout for the team that drafted me and worked a deal for me to go to their A team. It led to lots of bad blood between…well, all of us."

Maggie grimaced. "Ouch."

"So I left home and didn't talk to my mother for five years."

"But she was just being a mother. It's a dangerous sport. I can see why your mother…and even Charlie might want you to do something safer."

Like a match tossed into diesel fuel, anger exploded inside him. "No one is going to tell me how to run my life, and no one is going to tell me when I'm done riding. Not a stubborn old drunk or any woman. I can decide for myself when I should quit."

Maggie slid away from him, from the force of his anger. "I'm sorry. I was merely acknowledging their concerns. Surely you can see—"

"No," he interrupted, not wanting her to go any further explaining herself. She didn't get a say-so in his life.

"My decision to ride is mine alone. Gary and my mother overstepped. Charlie overstepped." He looked hard at her so she'd understand that she overstepped, too.

She tore her gaze away. "You're right. I shouldn't have brought it up."

He'd hurt her feelings, but he couldn't help it. Having his mother, Charlie and Gary try and stop him from doing what he loved had made him defensive. Better change the subject. "You going to get a pair of boots?"

Maggie looked down at the ones on her feet. "Think I'll take these."

"Good. I need to get the barrel. Told Wyatt he could help me install it tonight. You don't mind, do you?"

"Of course not. It will be nice to have some company at night." Her brown eyes went soft when she looked at him, making him feel like dog crap for blowing up on her. He shouldn't have dipped down into that emotional vortex. No need to have gone there. Should have told her it was nothing between him and Charlie. He had to remember that he and Maggie were temporary. They were shits and giggles. That was it.

"Let's mosey on, cowgirl," he said.

Maggie watched Cal instruct his younger brother in digging a two-foot hole with a posthole digger, still smarting from Cal's earlier outburst. She should have kept her mouth shut, but something inside her had wanted to help. Being a mediator was both her strong suit and her downfall.

Cal was installing the bucking barrel in the barn. He'd already unloaded five sacks of Sakrete he'd use to cement the pole in. The barrel sat over by the horse feed, covered with a tarp.

"Will this be removable? The new owners may need every stall," she asked.

Cal breathed hard after lifting the second bag of ready-mix cement. "We can get it out. No worries."

"Good," she said, eyeing the pregnant cat who peeked into the barn. The tabby darted green eyes left then right before gingerly stepping inside. A few seconds later, the cat leaped onto a stack of wood. For a heavily pregnant cat she was graceful.

"Why you selling this place, anyway?" Wyatt asked, lugging the bucket of water over to his brother. The lanky kid had hair that flopped into his face. Cal handed him a bandanna, inclining his head toward the sweaty mess.

"Because I don't live here." Maggie slid a little closer to the cat, hoping it might accept her presence better if she didn't look at it.

"But it would be a good place to live," Wyatt said, securing the bandanna and starting the slow pour into the dusty cement Cal had poured into the hole. "I'd love it out here."

"It's nice," Maggie agreed, taking a few more steps. The cat stayed put but looked wary. "But I'm not the kind of gal to live on a ranch."

"Oh, a city girl, huh?" Wyatt said, watching his brother's hand for the stop motion. "Hannah's like that. I mean, she wants to go to college in Houston. Says she's tired of staring at the same ol' people. Me? I'm happy here. I mean, I'm going to college and all, but I like living in a small town. Coyote Creek's kinda boring, but it's nice. Right, Cal?"

Cal shrugged.

Wyatt looked up. "You're going to move back here, aren't you? I mean, when you quit riding and stuff."

Cal looked up. "I don't know. Never thought about it."

Maggie could hear the aggravation in his voice. The man didn't want to talk about his future. But the future weighed heavy on her mind. She needed to get a plan together for a consulting business, but first she'd have to sell the ranch. If she had to get a job in between she would.

Should she stay in Philly or move to where her mother and aunt lived? It sounded lonely. But she'd find somebody. At least a roommate or something. She didn't have a lot of friends. So many of her college roommates had already married or advanced in their careers. They'd moved on. Her job at Edelman Enterprises had kept her in a pickle as far as making friends. She didn't necessarily have seniority over everyone, but she'd had Bud's ear and respect. She'd been like the teacher's pet. Or Bud's mole. No one trusted her enough to invite her for drinks or chat her up at the cooler.

"You should come back here. You're not too old to start a new job or something," Wyatt said, grabbing the shovel and patting down the slimy-looking mixture.

"Thanks, kid," Cal said, catching Maggie's eye.

Maggie smiled. "He's right. You're not that old."

Cal sighed. "You two are bustin' my balls over this."

"I'm doing no such thing," Maggie said, stifling her smile. "I'm merely stressing that you're not old. I almost bought you Geritol the other day, but then I thought, he's not even forty years old yet."

Cal gave her a flat look. "Thanks, Mags."

Wyatt grinned. "You two are good together."

And that statement made her feel like she'd tipped

over the summit of a roller coaster and plunged down. Because they weren't supposed to be a couple. Not really.

Cal glanced up, his gaze meeting hers. Something flashed between them. Maybe it was an acceptance. Or maybe it was a desire for things to be different. For them to be more than a right now. A start to something that would last longer than a month more. Maybe it was acknowledgment of what they shared in spite of their pre-set rules of engagement. Or maybe Maggie had started wanting him to feel the way she felt.

Thing was, she wasn't sure exactly how she felt.

The future was a tricky thing and that old saying about the best laid plan of mice and men echoed in her mind.

"Help me unwrap the barrel and then I'll show you how to tie the rope. There are a couple of ways to do it. Some cowboys prefer it tight. Others don't like the idea of getting stuck and unable to dismount."

"Think I'll go with tight. I've been watching Chris Henry and he said it gives better results."

"Every cowboy has to decide for himself, but what you will do is wear a helmet. Mom will have a shit fit if you don't. And you don't want to see that," Cal said.

Maggie moved a little closer to the cat. It flinched and then leaped from the pile onto the barn floor, jetting out the open door quick as lightning. "Dang it."

Cal laughed. "Did you say 'dang it'?"

"Yes. I want to get that cat to trust me. She's stubborn as you are."

"Takes time," Cal remarked, walking over to the tarp and unhooking the bungee cords covering it. "But I like the way you talk Texan."

"When in Coyote Creek…" Maggie started for the

open door, following the wary feline. "I'm going to leave you boys to talk rodeo. I have to clean up some paint rollers and then fix something to eat. Wyatt, did you have supper?"

"Yes, ma'am. Mom and I went by the Barbwire Grill before we went to the Co-op. I'm good."

Yes, ma'am. So she was that old now. Or maybe ma'am was Wyatt's natural response. She'd noted Texans, young or old, were abnormally respectful of women. She'd been *yes, ma'am*'d and *no, ma'am*'d to death. "Then I'll say good night."

"I'll be in later," Cal said, giving her a wink.

He said it so easily. Like it was a given they were together. That they had something more than mere hot sex.

Misleading.

Her heart tore a little at the thought of this fabricated life they'd built over the past several weeks. Which was not good.

She glanced back at Cal's head bent next to his brother as they tamped and double-checked the position of the pole, and her insides went soft.

In spite of herself, she was falling for a cowboy.

And it would lead nowhere.

11

CAL LEANED BACK against the headboard. "Baby, you were made for wearing cowboy boots."

Maggie's smile had the devil in it. She walked back and forth, strutting in her new boots, wearing nothing but a lacy bra and thong panties. Every fantasy a man could ever have sashayed in front of him.

She grabbed his cowboy hat off the bedpost and jabbed it on her head. "There. Now I'm a real cowgirl."

"Damn, girl. Come over here and let me see what kinda cowgirl you are." Cal leaned up and reached for her, but she scooted away.

"Oh, no, bull rider. I'm here for the lessons."

He gave her a slow smile. "Oh, are you? Well, thing is, I expect payment up front."

She turned and stuck her hands on her hip bones. "That doesn't seem fair. I've always demanded service rendered before I open my checkbook."

"Is that right?" he asked, reaching for his belt buckle.

Wyatt had left an hour ago, and Cal had come inside to find Maggie eating popcorn and drinking wine. A weird combination, but he'd joined her. One bottle led to tequila after she said she'd never done tequila shots. Like he could let her leave Texas without shooting authentic Mexican tequila. They'd both gotten a little sloppy and then turned on when he brought up giving her private lessons on riding a bull.

"Mmm-hmm. I must stand firm on these negotiations," she said, sliding her gaze down to the zipper he was in the process of lowering.

"Speaking of firm," he said, shucking his worn Levi's and tossing them toward the old rocker in the corner. He was left clad in his tented boxers and a pair of black socks. He looked like a turned-on nerd. But whatever. He couldn't think about what he was or wasn't wearing when Maggie pranced around, bouncing in all the right places.

"Now that's a look," she said, eyeing the erection standing tall beneath the material.

"No, that's good preparation. The first thing you want to do is rosin up your hands. Here, use this." He tossed her the lube she'd left sitting on the nightstand. Not that she'd needed it yet. He made damn sure she didn't need any lubricant in bed.

"This isn't rosin."

"Well, darling, you aren't going to be holding on to a scratchy rope now, are you?"

Maggie smiled and flipped the cap open. "But my bull doesn't look ready to ride."

Cal glanced down at his cock saluting her. "I beg your pardon?"

"Take those boxers off. The socks, too."

"Yes, ma'am."

"Those words again. You Texans love to call everyone ma'am."

Cal grinned and slid his boxers off. Socks joined them on the floor. Then he stacked some pillows behind his head and lay back. "Minding one's manners around here is a necessity. Not doing so can land a kid an ass whuppin', so we learn early."

Maggie squirted some lube in her hand and strolled over. "Mmm-hmm. We'll talk about manners later. Right now your role is to teach me how to hang on to a big, throbbing…uh, bull."

He would have laughed, but she chose that moment to wrap her slick fingers around his…bull. "Sweet mother of—"

"Am I doing it right?" she asked, looking innocent and wicked at the same time. She started moving her hand up and down. "I guess I should find a good spot to hang on. Here? Or right here?"

He gritted his teeth so he wouldn't come right there in her hand. The slick lube combined with the friction felt ten times more pleasurable than a normal hand job. "You're doing fine," he managed.

"Good. I want to learn how a real cowgirl does it."

"You're doing damn fine," he managed. He closed his eyes and spent a few seconds enjoying her ministrations. Because they were good. Her hands on his body, the way her breath ratcheted and the feel of her bared thigh on his arm made him feel out of control.

His Maggie knew what she was about.

That thought startled him. He'd never thought of a woman in those terms. And he shouldn't now because Maggie didn't belong to him or Texas. She'd wear the boots for a while. She'd ride the cowboy for a while. Then she'd go back to Philly, set the boots in the back of her closet to collect dust. And he'd be "that one time when I owned a ranch for two months" memory in the back of her mind.

For some reason the thought of her forgetting him bothered him.

He caught her hand, tossing out any serious thoughts. Time for Miss Maggie to get her ride on. "Your hands are ready. Let's go over some basics."

"Okay."

"First you'll need the right equipment." He eyed her lush breasts, the dark areolas visible through the silver lace. "Never mind, I can see you've got the equipment."

Her giggle made her breasts bounce slightly. Another good reason to make her laugh. Jiggly parts.

"Now, let's talk about mounting up. The bull will be in the chute, ready to go. You need to be wary of climbing on. There are things that could go wrong. The bull could get aggravated and…blow his load."

"Really?" Maggie asked.

"I'm struggling with the analogy," he said, caressing her hip. She slapped his hand away with a look of warning. Role play. Right. "In actuality the bull is pissed off. Me? I'm just turned the hell on."

"So let's try this," she said, sliding her panties off, presenting him with her rounded ass.

He groaned at the lush sight.

"What?" she asked. She turned around and his eyes zeroed in on the trimmed strip of hair covering the sweetest of prizes. Better than a gold buckle. He gripped the bed so he wouldn't touch her.

"This is torture," he croaked.

"Should I go ahead and mount?"

"Yes. Please." She set her knee on the bed, opening

her thighs enough so he could see the puffed lips of her sex. He dug his fingers into the mattress harder.

"Does it help to touch the bull?" she asked, swinging one leg over him so she straddled his thighs. She still wore the boots and hat. Her breasts spilled over the lace of her bra and her firm thighs on either side, pubis thrust toward him, was the hottest thing he'd ever seen. Seriously. Hottest thing ever.

"Uh, usually not. But in this case…"

She trailed a soothing hand down his chest and abs. "Good boy."

Cal managed a choked laugh. "You're killing me."

"Next, I grab the rope, right?"

"Uh, there's no rope, baby."

"So let's pretend." She clasped his cock and eased toward it. Maneuvering the tip, she brushed her clitoris. "Oh, yes, that's nice."

Understatement.

Her head dropped back, the cowboy hat nearly coming off. Her brown hair tumbled down her back as she moved her hips, using the head of his cock to circle her clit. Wicked hot heat singed him.

Her breath came hard. "Is this okay? Am I doing it right? 'Cause it feels right. It feels so good."

"You're doing fine," he said, reaching up to clasp her hips. He wanted inside her, but he loved watching her pleasure herself.

"Just a sec," she said, shimmying over to snatch something from the table. She held the condom package up. "You almost forgot about this."

Shit. He never forgot a condom, not even when drunk. Maggie had swept him away so completely he wasn't himself.

She made quick work of getting him sheathed. "There. I'm sure it's important that the bull is always protected. Animal welfare and all that." Clasping the base of his cock, she lifted herself and sank down on him.

Cal groaned at both the unexpected move and the sheer pleasure of being enveloped by her tightness.

"I'm on," she trilled, her grin triumphant and naughty. "Instruct me."

He didn't want to play anymore. He wanted to fuck. But he always finished what he started, so he lifted his hips. "Let's make sure you're on good."

She squealed a little and then closed her eyes. "Oh, I'm on good. Very good."

"Okay, now what you have to realize is the bull has a mind of his own and his goal is to get you off."

"That's my goal, too," she teased.

Cal grinned. "And so you try to anticipate his moves so you can stay on."

"So I can get off," she joked.

"Okay, cowgirl, hold on." He bucked his hips, moving to the left, then to the right. "Now you try and stay on. And it might help if you move with the bull."

Maggie nodded and moved her hips, riding him. She paused only a moment to reach behind her back and release her gorgeous breasts from the bra that held them captive. They were full, rounded, perfectly tipped orbs of some kind of something he didn't have words for because he was too busy feeling the tight, beautifulness that was Maggie. But he could damn sure appreciate perfection. He thrust, grinding his hips, pretending he was a bull so his cowgirl could get her ride on. Her breasts bounced, her delicious brown waves swayed and her face was screwed in concentration.

Then she leaned forward, placing each hand on either side of his head. Her breasts fell against his chin and she lifted one foot and planted it beside his hip. Then she started moving, lifting her body and sinking down onto his cock. He filled his mouth with one of her nipples, sucking hard, nipping with his teeth. She groaned and increased her speed, her lips brushing his jaw with small, sweet kisses. She bit his earlobe and whispered, "You don't seem like you're interested in bucking me off anymore."

He released her breast so it slapped his chest. "If bulls were ridden like this, I'm sure they wouldn't be interested in getting free, either. You're amazing," he said, his balls tightening as the pressure built. He was close to exploding...but Maggie hadn't come yet. And he was a Texas gentleman so he pushed her upright so she sat astride him again, and gently parted the folds of her sex, finding the bud of her clitoris. Wetting his thumb with her slickness, he began slow, steady circles.

"Oh," she said, her head falling back. "That's so good."

"So come for me, baby. I want to watch you ride me and come." He increased the tempo, loving the sight of her so open to him. She was pink, lush and so very feminine—a visual feast any red-blooded man could appreciate.

Only took a few seconds before he felt her tighten, the muscles inside her pulling at his cock as she found her release.

"Oh, oh, oh," she said, her eyes closed, her mouth open. But the trembling of her hips paired with the contractions sent him over the edge. He clasped her hips, moving her, and came in a hot torrent of wonderfulness. Maggie went limp and collapsed on his torso.

Cal kept moving until he was empty and then he fell still, savoring the feel of her body covering his.

He wound his arms around her, dropping a kiss on her sweaty cheek. "You're a good student."

She laughed. "I held on…and got off."

"Mmm-hmm. And you can ride me anytime."

"Bet you say that to all the girls," she said against his neck, dropping a kiss against the scruff he'd neglected to shave that morning because they'd spent too much time in the shower. His hunger for her was insatiable, like nothing he'd ever experienced. He didn't understand why he felt this way, why he wanted to breathe her in twenty-four hours a day. And it wasn't just sex. It was eating cereal with her, working beside her as she painted, cleaned, dug up flower beds. For the first time in forever, his feet didn't itch…and even worse, he didn't hunger for the dust of the arena, the smell of sweat or the cold beer waiting at the end of each night.

And that scared him down to the marrow in his bones.

Because he didn't feel hungry anymore.

Because he'd started wondering what it might be like to let the life he'd led slip away, fade behind him.

Because, for the first time in his life, he wondered what it would be like to sink into a recliner and watch the game, plant some tomatoes and watch them grow, and make a mortgage payment and not worry about what bull he drew or practicing or reserving a hotel room in Dallas.

"Stay with me," she whispered, sliding off him and curling next to his side.

They were the same words she'd whispered every night, the words he loved to hear. "You bet."

A FEW DAYS later Maggie watched Cal adjust the rope for Wyatt. The bucking barrel was ready and Cal's kid brother looked like Christmas had come early.

"Start slow and work on tightening the muscles in your thighs as you move. You'll be sore tomorrow, but it will be a good sore," Cal said.

Wyatt nodded. "Can't be worse than the way I feel after two-a-days. Besides I've been practicing on Jamie Riggs's bucking barrel. I'm pretty good on it."

"We'll see," Cal said, handing Wyatt a helmet.

"Why do I have to wear this? We're practicing." Wyatt frowned at the helmet that looked part bike helmet, part lacrosse helmet.

"Because everything matters. You practice the way you ride."

"Got it," Wyatt said, shoving the helmet onto his head. "Guess after having your head kicked a bunch of times, you would know."

Those words made Maggie glance up at Cal. Had his head kicked? That sounded more than dangerous. He'd said his mother and Gary had issues with Wyatt riding, so why would Cal teach his younger brother something so dangerous? She'd done research on riding bulls, the PBR and injuries like the one Cal had sustained. She'd also read about Lane Frost and the other bull riders who'd met their death in the rodeo arena. Rodeo was not just dangerous. It was deadly. And the thought of Cal climbing onto the back of the bull who'd crushed him made her stomach sour. But then again, it was none of her business.

The pregnant barn cat meowed, drawing her mind away from the thought of Cal lying crumpled at the foot of a deadly animal.

Maggie had managed to lure the cat closer to her using canned tuna. She'd set it near the bucking barrel stall and spent several minutes inching closer. The cat seemed content to chow down. Maybe it was getting used to her.

"When can I get on a real bull?" Wyatt asked, sliding onto the apparatus that looked straight out of a playground sans the bright cartoon character.

"I called Hal and he said we could come out and try some of his yearlings. Let's see how you do with proper instruction first."

"Okay, but maybe next week? You'll be ready by then, huh? I heard you tell Mom that you were doing better than you thought at therapy," Wyatt said.

Maggie tore her gaze away from the cat. Over the past week, she'd watched Cal subconsciously rub his shoulder several times a day and pop pain pills. Several nights she'd woken to find the bed empty and Cal sitting on the old rocker, massaging his shoulder, his face etched in pain. Not exactly doing better.

"That's what I'm thinking," Cal said, assisting his younger brother in positioning the rope. His tone was confident…or perhaps wishful. Either way, Maggie doubted he told the whole truth.

The tabby lapped at the canned tuna, the smell making Maggie wrinkle her nose. She crept a bit closer, easing herself onto the barn floor. The cat paused and looked up at her. Meeting gazes, they both sat still, watching each other. After nearly a minute, the cat resumed eating. Maggie stayed where she was, watching Wyatt rock and roll on the pretend bull, listening to Cal instruct him, and trying to show the cat she would do no harm.

Looking around the barn, she marveled at the changes. Fresh paint and a good scrubbing had done wonders. They'd hauled away tons of old junk, including the ancient tractor, and Cal had rounded up all the tack and taken it to be cleaned and repaired.

Never in a million years had she ever imagined herself sitting cross-legged and content on the floor of a barn in Texas watching a man she lo—

No. She didn't love Cal. That was absurd.

Love wasn't something she knew about. Oh, sure, she loved her family and few close friends, but she'd never been in love. The relationships she'd had thus far had been pleasant at best, forced at worst. But never had love been part of it.

"Maggie," Cal called to her.

She tore her mind from thoughts of love. "What?"

"Come try the barrel," Wyatt said.

"I'm fine here. You keep practicing," she said, frowning as the cat finished her meal and slunk away. No petting her tonight.

"Come on, babe. I want to see if you can stay on. Don't worry, I'll give you the first lesson free." Cal gave her a wink.

Her heart jerked at the grin and teasing. The man knew very well she'd already taken her first lesson. Of course this one wouldn't end as pleasurably. "I don't want to show Wyatt up."

"Shit," Wyatt scoffed.

"Watch your language around a lady," Cal said.

"I ain't no lady," Maggie drawled in her best Mae West imitation.

"Sorry, Maggie," Wyatt said, sliding his eyes away, looking abashed. "He's right. I'm not supposed to be cussing around girls."

"You Texans kill me," Maggie said, shaking her head. Lifting her leg over the barrel, she made to leap up. Cal caught her around the waist and set her on the back of the bucking barrel.

"Why? 'Cause we treat a lady like a lady?" Cal said, helping to guide her hand into the slack area in the knotted rope.

"Yeah, and I've never seen people who identify themselves so much by the state they live in," she said, wiggling until she felt steady on the bucking bull.

"We can be a little obnoxious about it," Cal said, stepping back. "Let's see what you can do, cowgirl."

Maggie started moving, stiffening up when the barrel shifted to the front. Felt like riding a slinky. "This is hard."

"That's what she sa…" Wyatt pressed his mouth together, making Maggie laugh. But not for long. She tightened her thighs and shifted in the other direction. The barrel went with her.

"Arm up," Cal shouted, steadying her with his big hands. She liked the way they felt on her, guiding her as she tried to ride the glorified playground apparatus. "Now move with the bull."

She tried to move with the barrel, but she'd had too many days of lounging and not enough days at the gym. Her core was weak and her thighs felt like jelly. No wonder Cal had abs of steel. "Okay, enough," she said.

Cal pulled her off the barrel and into his arms. Leaning down he kissed her nose before releasing her. "Good job for a city girl."

"You know, Cal, you really ought to buy this place from Maggie," Wyatt said.

Cal straightened. "Got no use for it."

"You could train cowboys here, like a rodeo school. Or you could raise stock. Lots of cowboys do that. Remember Scotty Dawes? That's what he does now and his bull is up for Bull of the Year."

"I know damn well what Scotty does. His goddamned bull was the one who caused this." Cal pointed toward his injured shoulder.

"Jeez, I was making talk. Don't get your panties in a wad," Wyatt said, immediately bristling.

"Don't worry about what I'm going to do once I'm washed up. I'll manage."

Maggie shuffled back toward the barn door, not wanting to be part of this conversation. She'd already seen his reaction to meddling when they were at the Co-op. It was obvious Cal avoided thinking about his future after walking away from the PBR. And since their own arrangement would expire soon, there was no need to look ahead to anything more than what they would grill that night or whether they should paint the bathroom the same color as the bedroom. Essentially, she and Cal were Mr. and Mrs. Right Now.

No future.

"I didn't say you were washed up, Cal. You're puttin' words in my mouth."

Cal didn't say anything.

"Mom said we'd try to make Vegas this year."

Cal glanced up with surprise, a smile curving his mouth.

Maggie turned away at the sudden tears that sprang to her eyes. Not at Cal's response to his brother's declaration, but because it was further proof his life would go on without her. By the time he went to Mobile, she'd be wrapping up things here in Coyote Creek. She'd be moving on…if she could sell the place. Money had disappeared from her savings account like rain on a dry pasture.

She blinked the moisture from her eyes, determined not to be maudlin over life marching on, and nearly knocked over Charlie.

The old cowboy steadied her and said, "Good news. Think I found a buyer for this place."

12

CAL HATED THE potential buyer, Hunt Turner, on sight. For one thing the man was from Alabama. For another, he was tall, fit and looked like Clint Eastwood. And the deal breaker was the way he looked at Maggie. Like he judged good horseflesh and found her to his liking.

Hunt had stopped at a gas station almost a week ago and inquired about spreads for sale around the area. Luckily, Charlie had been at the Stop-N-Go buying a few things (aka beer) and overheard his conversation with the cashier. Charlie took the man's custom-made card with a fancy-sounding corporation imprinted under the name Hunter Clayton Turner, Jr.

Cal bet the man didn't know a cow from a steer. Probably had his boots hand tooled in Italy or something stupid like that.

"I like what you've done with the house so far," Hunt said, nodding at the freshly painted bathroom. "Nice fixtures, clean lines."

"A soaker tub will go here. Cal's tiling halfway up the wall with the most gorgeous green tiles you've ever seen. Whoever's soaking in the bubble bath will have a perfect view of the backyard. Once I get those roses put in along the white fence, it will be such a pretty vista. Are you married, Mr. Turner?" Maggie asked.

"Not any longer, but I'm looking to settle down. That's why I'm interested in the place. Putting down roots in a small town is important to me," he said, taking Maggie's elbow as she stepped over the boxes of tile Cal had stacked there yesterday. They were supposed to have begun the project that morning, but Hunt Turner called and asked to stop by before he drove back to Alabama. The man's big hands on Maggie's arm irritated the hell out of Cal.

"Why Texas?" Cal asked.

"Why not?" Hunt answered, giving nothing away.

"Because you're from Alabama," Cal sniped.

Hunt's lips twitched. "Guess that's true, but my grandfather was from Texas and I have good memories here. Besides, my business interests have shifted over the past few years. Moving closer to where I work makes sense."

"What's your business?"

"Oil and gas."

Of course it was. Not only was the man abnormally decent looking, but he likely had millions wasting away in some bank somewhere. "That's a volatile business, huh? Up and down."

"That's true," Hunt said, pausing at the door, allowing Maggie to exit first. Probably so he could check out how incredible her ass looked in the short skirt she'd pressed that morning. She wore her hair in a braid and a bright blue shirt that hugged her curves. And those cowboy boots. Damn, she looked like a Southern dream in those cowboy boots.

"Next is the barn. After you've seen it and the outer buildings, Cal will drive you out to look at the land. He can answer your questions in regards to livestock, property lines and what have you," Maggie said, using a professional voice. Like she answered phones or something. But her smile was more genuine than polite.

"Thank you, Maggie," Hunt said, following her out into the living area.

"I hate you have to see the place mid-renovation," Maggie said, turning and gesturing to the fireplace. "We're still in the process of installing a new mantel and you can see the wood we're using for the floors. It's a nice stained oak."

"No worries," Hunt said, his eyes on Maggie's breasts. Or maybe not. Cal couldn't tell. Hunt seemed a sneaky devil, the kind of man who could ogle boobs but not get caught at it. "I can see it will be nice once it's completed. I like the kitchen floor."

"Thank you. We thought it contrasted nicely with the white cabinets and quartz counters." Maggie's amber eyes glinted with pride. Her gaze met Cal's and damned if her pleasure over how nicely the kitchen they'd designed turned out didn't make his heart swell. Not to mention during the entire tour she'd said "we did this" or "we thought that." Never *I*. Always *we*. As if they were a team. He hoped it gave Mr. Cadillac Fancy Pants the firm idea Maggie wasn't up for grabs.

Only the Triple J.

And even that bothered him.

Ever since Wyatt had suggested he buy the place, he'd been flipping the idea over in his head. He had unfinished business and wanted that million-dollar purse. But some day he'd have to do something else. And when he did, why not do as his brother suggested? Bull riding school. He knew there were a few decent bull riding schools around the country, but there was only one in the whole state of Texas. Maybe he could raise bulls and conduct some sessions on bull riding at the same time. The bunkhouse could easily be converted into dormitories and the spread was the perfect size for both endeavors. It could work. In fact, it could work really well.

But he didn't have a couple of million lying around to make something like that happen. Sure, he had made good investments, thanks to his stepfather, but he didn't have much liquidity. Still, a sound business plan could net him a loan. He had the name recognition to pull it off and if he could hire a few other decent bull riders, he'd be a shoe-in trainer for up-and-comers. Maybe he'd talk to Gary and see what his stepfather thought. Gary might even see it as an investment opportunity. Cal would have to put pen to paper and see what he could come up with before he broached the subject over Sunday dinner.

"Should we go to the barn?" Maggie asked, walking toward the front door. "It's in great shape. Do you own horses, Mr. Turner?"

"We have two Irish Sport horses, but I also have a few quarter horses. My daughter shows."

"Oh, you have a daughter," Maggie said, raising her eyebrows.

Hunt smiled, following her onto the porch. "Sara's passionate about her horses."

"How old is she?"

"Ten." Hunt wasn't very forthcoming, but that suited Cal fine. He didn't want the man getting chummy with Maggie any more than he had to. In fact, he didn't want to show him the acreage. Hunt needed to leave and forget about Maggie and the Triple J.

Adios, Bama.

"What a fun age," Maggie said, beaming at Hunt. "I remember when I was ten. So curious about the world, but still so innocent. Treasure that."

"I do. I wasn't around much when she was younger, so I'm trying to make it up to her. Fresh start."

Something in his tone made Cal soften slightly toward the man. Sounded like regret and Cal could understand that. He'd not spoken to his mother for the first part of Wyatt's life so he felt he hardly knew the sometimes sullen, sometimes enthusiastic teenager who'd sat across from him at the breakfast table the whole month of June. That realization was one of the reasons he'd agreed to teach Wyatt how to ride a bull. Before the accident and surgery, Cal had dreaded the thought of being in Coyote Creek, stuck in bed at the Whitehorse house. He hadn't wanted to intrude on a family that didn't feel his, especially when he knew he'd be in pain.

Over the past few weeks of loving Maggie every night and spending time with his brother, Cal had found life in Coyote Creek not as painful as anticipated.

"A fresh start," Maggie repeated, nodding her head. "Sounds like a perfect plan."

Fifteen minutes later, they stood in front of Cal's pickup. The old horse Maggie now called Sissy nickered at the fence, looking not as pathetic as she once did. Or maybe she did, but Cal now saw her through a different lens.

"I haven't seen the land yet, but I already know I'm interested," Hunt said, setting his hands on his lean hips and perusing the house and surrounding buildings. "It's the perfect size for my needs and it's not too fussy. Feels like a real home."

Maggie looked over at the house, something sparking in her eyes. "Yes, it's very much like a real home."

Her words sounded sad. Was she regretting her decision to sell? Part of him wanted her to. Because something inside him wanted her to choose him, to stay in Texas and fight for what they had between them. But it wasn't fair of him to wish that. Not when he knew he couldn't—no, that he *wouldn't*—commit to a future.

He had his eye on the prize and that prize was in Las Vegas.

Cal would finish the business he had before he faced the monster that nipped at his heels…let go of who he'd always been.

A few days ago he'd gone in for an MRI on his shoulder. The doctor had left a message on his phone in a voice that left little room for doubt. Early on they'd discussed the possibility of a second surgery and now Cal knew the possibility was a reality. A tear in his rotator cuff needed to be repaired in order for him to have full rotation of his arm. Cal had likely overtaxed his shoulder too soon after the original surgery. His enthusiasm for getting stronger had led to redamaging the ligaments. The tiny tear was the reason he still had to pop half a pain pill a couple of times a day. Of course, even with the tear, Cal could finish the season. Riding that way would mean a steady diet of medication and therapy. He'd have to compensate for the inflexibility. Climbing in the rankings would be doubly hard. But Cal could do it.

"Cal?" Hunt said, turning toward him.

"Yeah."

"Maggie said you'd drive me around?" Hunt asked.

Cal gestured toward his truck. "Sure."

Maggie's forehead furrowed at his clipped reply. Couldn't the woman see the guy's slimy gaze on her? Didn't she realize Cal was obliged to warn the man off? Did she know she was Cal's? At least his for almost three more weeks.

When Hunt glanced back, Maggie summoned a cheerful smile. "See y'all when you get back."

"Did you just say 'y'all'?" Cal asked.

She blinked, looking surprised before laughing. "Well, when in Texas."

She'd said those words several times before. As if being in Texas was like a magic pass to do things she'd never do again. Like wear cowboy boots. Shoot tequila. Ride a cowboy. It was as if saying "when in Texas" made everything they'd been doing for the past weeks a mere lark. Not real.

Thing was, everything felt too real to Cal. Like a lit match tossed in gasoline, he and Maggie had gotten explosive fast. Which was maybe why he felt like an old porch dog, growling and pacing the perimeter, refusing to let Hunt Turner take a sniff. Perhaps it was time for Cal to pull back and get perspective.

But then Maggie looked at him expectantly with eyes so full of question, cheeks flushed from the heat and mouth curved in a pseudosmile that said she understood why he was acting like an enormous ass. And he knew he couldn't step away.

Only two weeks, five days and a handful of hours left until he headed to Mobile, shoulder healed or not.

Only two weeks, five days and a handful of hours left until he walked away from Maggie.

"Cal," Hunt said again.

"Huh?"

"Ready?" the man said, looking far too cool in the Texas afternoon heat.

No. He wasn't ready. "Sorry. This heat is making me punchy."

Hunt narrowed his eyes in concern. Like maybe he didn't want to climb into a big 4x4 with a dude who admitted to being affected by the heat.

"Don't worry. I'm fine."

But the truth was he wasn't fine. He was just a good liar. Because his shoulder was screwed and his heart teetered on Heartbreak Ridge. And Cal knew that when he left Coyote Creek, it wouldn't be the way he'd hoped months ago when he told his mother he was coming home to heal.

MAGGIE WATCHED CAL drive off with Hunt Turner and sighed.

She had her first bite on the ranch…maybe soon to be followed by a genuine offer. So why didn't she feel as though an enormous burden was about to be lifted from her? Good Lord, a potential buyer had dropped into her lap. Wasn't selling the Triple J quickly what she'd wanted all along?

Her tummy trembled at the thought of handing over the keys to the place.

Maybe it was natural to feel the way she did. After all, she'd been working hard over the past weeks. Pouring sweat into a project of this scale connected a person to it. No doubt all the house flippers on those TV shows also got attached to their projects. Maybe at some point they wanted to take a broom and shoo buyers away, too.

She climbed the porch steps and eyed the paint she'd

set out. She'd already put a coat of sky blue on the porch roof to fool the bugs. One more coat and she could start on the railing. She'd roll the protectant on the new porch decking the day after. It would be a gorgeous spot to hang a porch swing and a couple of Boston ferns. A perfect spot to find peace and comfort.

The Triple J was starting to look like the place Bud had loved so. When she was a child she would look at the photographs of the Texas countryside framed in Bud's office. Her mother didn't like her going in there, but she loved to lie on the stuffy leather couch and look at the photos of bluebonnets and old fences with sunsets in the background. Her favorite had been the one of a longhorn cow staring directly into the lens. She'd wiggled on the couch, wondering if she could do a chinup on his horn or if the friendly looking bovine would poke her eye out if she tried. Bud had caught her in there one day staring at his photos and had begun to tell her stories about cows getting stuck in flooded creek beds, coyotes baying at moons and wide-open space to contemplate one's place in the big world. He'd say, *I'll take you there one day, kid. You can ride a pony and I'll show you the hanging tree.*

But he'd never taken her. Business took a downturn with a product recall and she'd grown into a teenager who stopped sneaking into Bud's home office.

Is that why he'd left the Triple J to her? Because he'd promised to take the housekeeper's bastard child and hadn't gotten around to it? Or because he wanted to poke a stick at his own kids who rarely visited him for anything other than a check?

No matter the reason, the Triple J was hers...for now. Fresh start.

Those words uttered by Hunt Turner stirred something in her. What if the Triple J was where she belonged… what if it was her own fresh start?

Years ago, hundreds of people had tossed practicality out the window to chase a dream out West. They'd broken away from their past to claim a dangerous future in a wild land full of rattlesnakes and sexy cowboys. Maybe she should be as bold. Maybe…

Cal's truck crested the slight rise that blocked the view of the highway, jarring Maggie from her thoughts. *Be sensible, Mags.*

But even as she told herself those words, she recalled something Bud once told her. *I found myself, this hard-nosed capitalist, this practical man, staring out at a horizon that sparked a sense of belonging. That land stirred the imagination, that land spoke to the heart. I met myself there, Maggie. I'm ten times the man when I'm riding a horse across the Triple J than when I'm nit-picking budgets here in Philadelphia. A place like that can change you. Make you believe God is real and you have a purpose.*

Maggie looked out over the land Bud loved so and knew what the old man had meant. Ever since she'd come to the Triple J, she'd felt more herself.

Or maybe that was because of Cal.

Nothing is etched in stone.

Cal climbed out of his truck and set his cowboy hat back on his head. He squinted toward the paddock where Sissy gnawed at dry grass. She didn't know whether he was trying to mind his own business or if he was worried about the horse.

Hunt headed toward Maggie. Holding out his hand, he said, "Thanks for showing me the Triple J. I'm going to sit down with my financial advisor and work out a few details. You should have an offer from me on the place by the beginning of next week. If anyone else comes to look at it or makes an offer, call me."

His handshake was firm and dry. Intentional. "I haven't listed with an agent yet, so I don't anticipate another offer yet."

"Good," Hunt said, giving her a smile. He was insanely attractive in a rough around the edges way. If she weren't so much in lo—

She clamped down once again on that thought. Because she wasn't in love with Cal. She couldn't be. Because they'd set rules and made plans to the contrary. She had to stop allowing that thought to slip into her subconscious. To think that way, to claim that emotion, was dangerous. Because love would lead to heartbreak. Despite her fanciful what-ifs, she knew what they'd set in place made sense. It protected both of them. Cal would return to his world and she'd…well, it was safe to bet she'd return to hers. There was no room for her to entertain anything different. Better to stick to the original plan—all the fun, none of the guilt. Like that yogurt commercial.

"It was a pleasure meeting you. If things don't work out with the Triple J, I wish you luck finding another place for your fresh start," Maggie said.

Hunt dropped her hand. "I think I've found it here. Sara will love it."

Cal made his way over and in his eyes she saw her doubt reflected. Or maybe it wasn't doubt as much as it was jealousy. She shouldn't feel so thrilled at Cal's response to Hunt, but she'd rarely experienced a man scratching a line in the dirt over her. Something about

Cal scowling at Hunt made her feel secure. It was a rarity, nothing more. But still, some part of her liked it too much.

Hunt extended his hand to Cal, gave it a brief, hard shake and then turned back toward his rental SUV. "I'll be in touch."

And then her potential buyer climbed into his vehicle and drove away.

"You're not going to let that asshole buy this place, are you?" Cal asked.

"Asshole?" Maggie repeated turning to Cal. "Come on, Cal, that man was perfectly nice. He has a daughter. He wants a fresh start."

Cal shook his head. "Naw, he's weird. I can tell he has secrets."

"Cal," she chided with a laugh.

"Seriously. Who picks up and moves to some place they've never been before? Unless they're a drug dealer...or an illegal arms dealer. He's trouble. I can smell it. There's something off about him. He could be a serial killer."

"You sound like a nut," Maggie said. His words made her earlier thoughts about staying in Coyote Creek seem ridiculous, too. Who, indeed, picks up and moves to a place she'd never been before? No one. Okay, some people but not ones who had common sense. There had to be a good reason to do something like that. Maggie had no good reason. She hadn't even broken in her new cowboy boots yet much less done any research on how to run a ranch. Better to ditch the itch, the idea, the inclination.

Maybe the heat was making her punchy, too.

"I *am* a nut," Cal said, grabbing hold of her and pulling her into his arms. "Over you."

Maggie let the decision drama slip away in favor of lightness. She didn't want to spend the time she had left with Cal overanalyzing every aspect of her future. No, she wanted to grab the pleasure she could. She'd think about bad decisions and potential heartache after she walked away from the Triple J and Cal.

That thought bumped against her bubble of happiness, but she flicked it away by kissing Cal. "I like nuts."

"I could make a dirty joke," he said, grinning down at her.

"As expected," she said, looping her arms around his waist and leaning back so she could stare up at him in the early afternoon sun. "I'd love to practice bull riding on you, but we have too much daylight left."

"You're a slave driver, woman. Can't take a single day for some fun."

"And if we were going to take the afternoon off, what kind of fun do you have in mind?" she said, suggestively bumping her hips against his.

"Skinny-dipping?"

"In the pond?" She wrinkled her nose.

"It is kind of stagnant," he conceded.

"Where's Wyatt?" she asked, realizing she hadn't seen the teen in a while.

"He's helping Charlie repair the fences out in the far pasture," Cal said, raising his brows in expectation.

"So no one is around?" she asked.

He shook his head. "What do you have up your sleeve, madam?"

"I've been thinking of power washing the house. I could grab the bikini I bought at the Penny Mart. Doesn't cover much but we could get wet." Maggie lowered her voice when she made the suggestion. No way was she shucking her clothes and jumping into a lukewarm pond filled with bacteria and algae, but she could be talked into some slippery fun. "We'll call it killing two birds with one stone. Work and play."

"A cheap bikini that doesn't cover much," he mused, stroking his chin. "Hmm…is that enough fun for the afternoon?"

"Or we can start tiling in the bathroom with all our clothes on," she suggested.

"Negatory. Last one to the…uh, water hose…is a rotten egg," he shouted, releasing her and bolting for the trailer where he still kept his clothes. And she presumed his swimsuit.

13

So much for tiling the master bathroom.

But wasn't kinky, wet fun with Cal worth losing an hour or two on the project?

With so little time left together, she'd have to give a resounding vote in favor of kinky, wet fun. And since it was hotter than a Fourth of July firecracker outside, cooling off was almost a safety precaution. In fact, health professionals should add a good soaking with the water hose to their pamphlets on how to avoid heatstroke. Bikini optional.

Maggie hurried toward the house, hoping like hell the power washer she'd hauled out of the barn still worked. Of course, she and Cal would have to get wet with the water hose and not the high-pressure spray. She didn't want to lose any skin. A nice trickle of cool water and splashing around with a near-naked Cal in the Texas sunshine would be a perfect way to distract her from the doubts that had crept up about selling the ranch.

Ten minutes later she emerged in the hot-pink monstrosity she'd bought last minute at the discount store in Coyote Creek. She had no clue why she'd tossed it into the shopping cart. She'd never worn a string bikini before and this one with its tiny scraps of fabric barely held her breasts. The bottoms tied together like an invitation. At the last minute she braided her hair on each side of her head like a farm girl. She looked like one part country music video and two parts white trash.

"Hot damn," Cal marveled when she emerged from the kitchen screen door, some parts of her bouncing more than others.

Cal wore a pair of cutoff shorts and nothing else. He looked like every teenage girl's dream, sipping a long-neck beer, wearing a pair of Ray-Ban aviator sunglasses.

"And it only cost ten dollars," she said, turning so he could see how little of her butt it covered.

"Worth every cent," he said, setting his empty beer on the back steps and walking around the side of the house to where the grass grew thick and cool under a shady tree. The power washer had been set up, but the garden hose scrolled through the yard like a lazy green ribbon. "Let's make sure the water works."

Cal turned the spigot and water gushed from the end of the hose. Picking it up, he tested the temperature. "It's warm."

Maggie stepped over and held out her hand, but Cal pulled the hose back and sprayed her with it.

It was not warm.

More like freezing.

Maggie shrieked. "You pig."

Cal laughed and hit her in the face with a full blast. She lunged toward him, grabbing his forearm and swinging her foot around to wrap around the hose. He jumped back in surprise, but she managed to wrench the hose from him.

"What's good for the goose is good for the gander," she said, sliding her hands toward the nozzle.

"What's a gander?" he asked, holding his hands up. Useless protection.

She put her thumb over the stream and wiggled her eyebrows.

"No, you don't," he said, reaching for her. But Maggie was quick and she managed to douse the front of his body with a good spray of water. "Ah! That's frickin' cold."

"I know," she squealed with delight.

Cal grabbed her around the waist and pulled her to him, but she slipped on the now-slick grass and fell on her butt. He tumbled down with her, pulling the hose so it blasted onto her naked belly.

"Crap," she gasped, pushing the hose away.

The heat of the afternoon paired with the cool water was actually a perfect combination. Maggie had never in her life played in the water hose. She'd never worn hoochie-mama bikinis or frolicked on the green grass with a sexy beast of a man, either. She found the whole silly escapade to her liking. And she liked it even more when Cal pulled her into his lap and kissed her.

Her nipples were hard from the cold water and they grew even tighter as they brushed his hard chest. His mouth was hot against her cold lips, chasing the chill away even as the icy water pooled beneath them, no doubt soaking Cal's worn cutoff blue jeans.

Cal cupped one of her breasts and squeezed, making heat spiral deep into her pelvis.

"That's nice," she whispered against his lips.

"Isn't it?" he whispered back.

Maggie shifted to the side and pulled a leg through

their bodies so she straddled him. The hose caught between them and poured over Cal's thighs, soaking her bikini bottom with icy water. She could feel that hard length of his erection pressing against her and the juxtaposition of the heat from Cal against the cold water was oddly erotic.

Cal kissed her again, his tongue hard and demanding against hers, stoking her desire for him, teasing with a nip to her lip before he pulled back and slid his sunglasses off, tossing them to the side. "This is the stupidest but maybe best idea I've ever had."

Maggie stuck her hands on her hips. "It was my idea."

"So it was, and damn if you ain't kinky, woman," he said, sliding the fabric of one pink triangle aside, freeing her breast. Smiling as if he'd found a treasure, Cal lowered his head to suck the nipple into his mouth. Maggie couldn't prevent the hiss that escaped her lips. His hot mouth on her chilled skin felt amazing.

She wriggled her bottom and pulled the hose from between them. "I'm soaked."

"Just how I like you," Cal said, giving her a hard kiss before tipping her out of his lap. She squealed when she landed on the squishy grass but didn't have time to think about any discomfort because Cal had come to his knees, his fingers busy untying the strings on either side of her bikini bottom. Pulling the fabric back, he smiled. "Even better."

Maggie tried to close her legs, but he pressed his hands against her inner thighs. "Cal, I'm all for playing around, but we're out in the open."

Cal looked around. "No one is here."

"But your brother could be back at any moment." She

pushed at his hands, not wanting to be so vulnerable in the harsh sunlight.

He shook his head. "I texted Charlie and told him to keep Wyatt busy until five o'clock. No *if*s, *and*s or *but*s about it. We're all alone, Miss Stanton. And I'm here to serve you."

She shook her head, but allowed him to part her legs. "This is crazy."

"You're the one who wanted to get wet," he said, tracing the trimmed hair along her slit. Her body trembled at the sensation. And then she relaxed, submitting to his touch, wanting his hands on her more than she wanted to protect her modesty.

"And I am," she murmured huskily.

"So I see. So I feel," he said, dragging a finger through her dampness, making her jump at the contact. "You're so beautiful, Mags."

She loved when he called her by that pet name.

He sucked his finger into his mouth. "And you taste good, baby. Give me more."

His words were like honey dripping over her, slowly covering any protests that anyone could happen upon them. Maggie let her legs fall open, offering herself to him.

Cal bent and dragged his tongue through her slick folds, making an *mmm* sound.

"You make me feel crazy…reckless," she said, clasping his head as he found her clit and started working her. Maggie closed her eyes and let Cal do what he wished. She had no power against the seduction he employed. Her body fell victim to his particularly talented mouth and the knowing fingers inserted inside her, crooking to thrust against that perfect spot that made her body hum. He pushed her knees up, opening her wider so he could work her easier. "Oh, my…oh, Cal. Please, please."

He lifted his head, murmuring, "That's right, baby. That's right."

She pulled his hair and shoved him back down between her thighs, making him laugh. But she didn't care. All she wanted at that moment built inside her, a sweet beautiful pressure that made her lengthen her muscles and point her toes as she reached for the earth-shattering climax.

And it came crashing hard, shaking her body. She clenched her teeth and arched her back, calling out Cal's name.

But he didn't stop. No. This cowboy kept holding on, loving her with his mouth, hands firm on her hips so she couldn't wriggle away. She didn't need him to say the words to know he wanted her shattering against his mouth again.

So she did.

After the waves subsided, she untangled her fingers from his hair and scrambled, pushing him back as she came up to her knees. "That was fun. Now it's your turn."

"But I want to fu—"

"And where's your condom, Mr. Lincoln?" she said, tugging the button of his jeans open. The zipper glided smooth as butter and in five seconds, she had his cut-offs mid-thigh and boxers down so his thick erection sprang toward her.

"You have a point," he managed to say when she took hold of his thickness, sliding her probably too-cool hand over the smooth shaft and wrapping her fingers around him. "I'll defer to you, boss."

"Good boy," Maggie said, bending over and licking the glistening droplet of ejaculate from the head of his cock.

"Oh, shit," he breathed, his hands threading through her hair. "That's fucking good, baby."

"Mmm-hmm," she murmured, sucking the smooth, rounded head into her mouth. His fingers pulled her hair from the braids, telling her all she needed to know about how her mouth felt on him. She started moving, taking all of his length into the heat of her mouth, applying the perfect pressure. He was large but not monstrous, which made giving him head pleasurable. She worked him, one hand cupping his balls while the other framed her lips, adding pressure. He bent forward, reaching for her ass, stroking, dipping his fingers into her slick heat. He played with her while she did her best to drive him insane.

Didn't take long until she felt his balls tighten in her hand.

"Oh, Maggie," he groaned between what sounded like gritted teeth. And then she felt the spurt of hot ejaculate. She pulled off and worked him with her hand, lifting her gaze to watch him come.

Cal closed his eyes, muscles quivering in his chest as he thrust his hips in time with her hand.

"Shit, woman," he said, finally opening brilliant blue eyes that were still dilated and halfway amazed. "You trying to kill me?"

"You think that was me trying to kill you?" she joked, rising, refastening the string bikini and looking for the towel she'd spied earlier. Finding it tossed over the clothesline, she snagged it and handed it to Cal. "Guess we better figure out how to hook this water hose into the sprayer."

He reassembled his clothing. "You want to work after *that*?"

Maggie crooked her head. "That's what I'm paying you for."

"I was thinking along the lines of a nap."

"Wrong," Maggie said, picking up the hose that still gushed water. She walked over and turned the spigot off. "I'm going to fetch a T-shirt to cover this. I'd die if your brother saw me looking like this."

"We must protect the innocent," he said, eyeing the pressure washer.

"If you remember, we caught him out here trying to score with his girlfriend. I doubt he's all that innocent," she cracked.

Cal put his fingers in his ears. "I can't hear you."

Maggie smiled and headed back toward the kitchen door, marveling she'd engaged in oral sex out in the open. She'd once watched porn in college in which three people had frolicked naked in the middle of a public park, and rather than find the scenario titillating, she'd been appalled anyone could have sex somewhere a passerby could happen upon them. But she'd allowed Cal to peel her bikini off and go down on her on a grassy patch in broad daylight right outside a God-fearin' town. That's what the man did to her. He took things she thought impossible and made them perfect.

Just as she pulled on the screen door handle, she heard the sound of a vehicle come up the drive.

"Holy crap," she muttered, scooting inside the kitchen, terror and relief mixing together. She peered out as the silver sedan came to a halt in the gravel. Five minutes earlier and whoever was driving would have bumbled into a real-life porno. Scrambling up the back kitchen stairs, Maggie made it to her room and into a tunic T-shirt dress and sandals in less than two minutes, setting records with her wardrobe change. She could do nothing about the messy, damp braids or the flush in her cheeks from her romp with Cal, but she was presentable.

Sort of.

The doorbell rang right as she stepped back into the living area, something that surprised her since she'd never actually tried the bell before. She pulled the door open to an older man standing on the freshly painted porch. He had coal-black hair gathered into a queue, wore a crisp pair of blue jeans, white dress shirt and a silver bolo tie. His craggy face was tan, his cheekbones proclaiming him Native American, but his eyes were stone gray and somewhat distant. He looked startled, though he'd been the one ringing the bell.

"Can I help you?" she asked, wondering if perhaps he, too, had heard about the ranch for sale. Two potential buyers within hours of each other?

"Is Cal Lincoln here?"

"Cal?"

"Yes, I need to talk with him."

"Okay," she said, feeling a wariness creeping over her. This man did not look friendly. He looked perturbed. Had Cal done something to him?

The man's mouth flattened with impatience. "Ma'am?"

"Who may I say is asking?" she asked, gripping the doorknob tightly. Perhaps she should shut the door, lock it and get Cal.

"Gary Whitehorse."

"Oh," she said, her mind registering the man as Wyatt's father…Cal's stepfather. She vaguely recalled Cal saying Gary Whitehorse had the personality of a wall. "Of course. Won't you come in?"

He followed her into the dim living area.

"Cal's outside preparing to power wash the outside of the house. Let me get him before he gets started and can't hear me call him," she said, turning to find Cal already strolling through the dining area. He must have heard the car pull up. Thankfully he'd pulled on a T-shirt. His flip-flops slapped the bottom of his feet and he frowned when he saw Gary. "Gary. What's wrong? Why—"

"You didn't come for Sunday dinner," Gary said.

"I told Mom I wouldn't make it." Cal looked confused or aggravated. He didn't seem to care for Gary showing up unannounced. "You came out here to bust my balls for not coming—"

"No," Gary interrupted, picking up a small bronze reproduction of a Remington piece showing a cowboy riding a bronco. He made a face and set it back down. "I'm leaving on a business trip for a month. I need to speak with you."

Cal eased toward the couch, putting some distance between him and Gary as if he expected bad news. "About?"

"Jared called. He said you hadn't returned his call. He's worried."

"You talked to my doctor? That's against the code thing or whatever. The HIPAA stuff."

"Your mother's listed on your paperwork. Besides she and Jared are old friends by now. He's patched you up enough. Your surgeon did not discuss any results with your mother, but he implied you need a second surgery and seems to have concerns about you going back to the rodeo. He was surprised you hadn't mentioned this to your family or to the PBR officials."

Cal's face shuttered. "I haven't talked to Mom or the PBR because there's no need. This isn't your business, Gary. Or my mother's. Jared shouldn't have called the house. I would have returned his call."

"You're making dangerous decisions. Your mother can't sleep at night for worrying about you and about the fact you're teaching your brother to do something that could get him seriously injured."

"You've got to be joking. My shoulder is fine," Cal said, slapping a hand against the shoulder. "She and I discussed Wyatt. I know what I'm doing."

Gary stared flatly at his stepson before shaking his head. "We've never been close, Cal, and in the past, things have been tense. Still, I care about you. You're expressly ignoring the advice of the medical professionals. Why don't you come to work for me?"

"This is bullshit. I don't want to work for you and I know my limitations. My shoulder is fine. Jared doesn't have the final say and he doesn't understand that—" Cal bit off his response, glancing over at Maggie as if he'd suddenly realized she was still in the room. "You don't have to worry with this, Mags. Go start power washing. I'll be there in a minute."

A dart of hurt hit her in the solar plexus. Cal didn't want her there for the conversation with his stepfather. Again, he'd proven he didn't want her involved in the things that really mattered to him. Things like his career and future. She was a five-week-long booty call. "Sure. Nice to meet you, Mr. Whitehorse."

Gary nodded. "My mind weighs heavy. I apologize if I was abrupt."

"It's fine. Safe travels," she said, leaving the room, allowing the kitchen door to swoosh shut behind her.

Her throat felt scratchy with emotion even as her mind turned over all Gary said. Cal professed his shoulder was fine, and though she had her own reservations about Cal's health and return to bull riding, the fact he needed more surgery to repair his shoulder was a surprise. Because Cal had said nothing. He'd downplayed every wince, hidden his pain from her.

Already it was August which meant Cal's first event in Alabama was just weeks away. He'd been practicing on the bucking barrel, but he often did that while she stayed inside working on one project or another. When she thought back on it, she could see he didn't want her there when he practiced. Was it because he had trouble? Or because he couldn't do it?

Tomorrow evening he and Wyatt were going over to a friend's ranch north of Fort Worth to practice on live bulls. He'd even written up a funny request-for-leave form he'd left by her cereal bowl that morning, joking about working overtime to make it up to her. And by *overtime* he meant in bed. He acted like a man near the end of recovery.

So why would he lie?

Pride?

Well, duh. Yeah. He was a dude. Men were notorious for allowing pride to break line in front of reason. That's why they drove around for hours before asking for directions. She'd always thought it strange Siri was a woman because most men ignored directional advice given by a woman. No doubt, Cal's stubborn pride about the frailty of his body prevented him from making the right decision. Her cowboy was a determined man on a mission to get back in the saddle…or rather on the back of a bull. He'd probably go to Mobile even if his arm was hanging by a thread. Common sense wasn't an option.

Still, Cal's decision was none of her business even if she wished he'd trust her enough to confide his fears. She had no authority to offer an opinion. Five-week booty call indeed.

SWALLOWING HER OWN PRIDE, she marched to the fridge and grabbed a beer. Voices raised in the living room. Or maybe it was only Cal. She set her phone on the dock, turned on "Uptown Funk" and parked her butt against the beveled edge of the marble counter and sipped the Texas craft-brewed beer she'd bought at the McKinney Walmart.

The kitchen door banged open and Cal stormed in, scaring Maggie to such a degree she dropped the bottle of beer.

"Goddamned nosy ass needs to stick to minding his own affairs and not mine," Cal said, ignoring the bottle pumping ale onto the floor and grabbing himself a fresh one out of the fridge.

Maggie didn't say anything. Merely scooped up the bottle and covered the spill with one of the new dish towels she'd ordered from Amazon. Seemed like staying quiet would be the best move, especially since she now knew her role.

She glanced up at Cal and he said pointedly, "I'm fine."

"I didn't ask," she said, trying to maintain a cool distance.

He stared at her for a few seconds. "Okay, fine, my surgeon said I had some scar tissue and a small tear in the rotator cuff. I can have that crap cleaned out later and the tear repaired. After I retire. If I ever retire. I might decide to ride until I'm eighty. It's my own goddamn business if I do." He slammed the half-empty bottle onto the new countertop.

Maggie didn't say anything.

"I guess you agree with Gary, huh?"

"Why would I?" she asked.

"Because my balance could be off. Because I'm rushing things. Because I could go out there, draw that fucking bull again and end up in the morgue."

Maggie shook her head. "I don't agree with him. But I understand his concern."

"Bullshit. He just doesn't want to listen to my mother whine about me being stupid. He thinks I'm going to lead Wyatt into bull riding."

"Are you?"

"No. The point of going to Hal Sawyer's is to scare the mess out of my brother. Sawyer'll tell Wyatt he doesn't have a chance in hell at riding in the PBR. I'm taking care of the kid. But, me, I'm *fine.*"

Maggie shrugged. "Okay."

"I'm *fine,*" Cal said again. As though maybe he was trying to convince himself.

At that moment, Maggie understood so much about Calhoun Lincoln. About his past, his present and his dreaded future…the thing he wanted most to avoid. It was all so understandable. He was afraid, vulnerable and refusing to see anything other than the fact he wanted to go on being the Cal he'd always been. But life didn't always care what someone wanted. Life bucked, twisted and stomped on a person's plans the way Rasputin had done to Cal months ago. That bull had crushed something Cal couldn't control and that was his body. Or maybe not. Maybe Cal knew his body better than an MRI did.

But Maggie couldn't make Cal see he could be wearing blinders...and neither could anyone else. If Cal couldn't be the bull rider he'd been for the past fifteen years, he would have to come to terms with it. On his own.

"So let's forget about this and finish washing the house. I've decided to repaint it. We saved enough on the appliances that we have room in the budget. You know what Realtors say—a fresh coat of paint does wonders for resale value." She started toward the back door.

Cal's hand stopped her. "I'm sorry."

"It's okay. I'm used to men's temper tantrums. Bud was infamous for them."

"Seriously," he said, folding her into his arms. "I don't want you to think I'm stupid. I don't have a death wish."

But if he couldn't ride at the top of his game, maybe he did. She couldn't stomach the thought of him lying crumpled. What it must have done to his mother. What it must do to every family member of every bull rider who had gone down with serious injury. Still these cowboys climbed on bulls every weekend. Every day. They strapped themselves down on dangerous animals and most of them didn't die. Most of them had scars, but they didn't die.

"I know you don't," she said.

"Thanks for not lecturing me."

Maggie stepped back. "I have no right to lecture you."

For a moment he looked genuinely confused. As if he wanted to say she did have the right. But then he caught himself. "Right. So let's get busy."

"We already did," she joked. She needed to lighten the mood and bring her sexy, aw-shucks, let's-fuck cowboy back. Because Maggie couldn't handle a Cal who hid his doubts, who got angry if ever questioned about his career. She wouldn't jump into that swimming pool, especially without floaties.

Cal seemed to understand, because he gave her what she wanted—a lopsided cowboy grin. "I could be talked into Water Hose Hijinks Part Deux."

"Oh, is that the name of the movie?" Maggie joked, giving him a pinch. "Because I'm no longer wearing a bikini."

"You don't need a bikini," he said, following her out the door into the sunshine. Into the pretend world they'd created, a world where hurt couldn't possibly touch them. Because they said it couldn't.

14

HAL SAWYER HAD been a bullfighter before his knees
gave out. Not wanting to leave the rodeo life he loved
so well, he bought some bull semen from the owners
of Disastrous D, two-time Bull of the Year and one of
the rankest, meanest sumbitches ever ridden. Hal im-
pregnated fifty cows on the ranch he bought from his
father-in-law and ended up with a crop of bulls that fre-
quently made appearances in the finals. His place was
fifty miles southeast of Coyote Creek, which was handy
for Cal's purposes. He wanted Wyatt to get started on a
young bull before taking a ride himself on one of Sawyer's best up-and-comer bulls.

"Here," he said, handing Wyatt one of his safety vests.
He'd been teaching Wyatt the proper way to spur the
bull, how to make sure the chaps were on correctly and
the technique for braiding his rope. He'd drilled the kid
on chute safety and how to dismount effectively. They'd
watched countless YouTube videos, slowing rides down to
point out mistakes. Cal still didn't think Wyatt was ready,
but he knew he had to let the kid try it all in real time.

"Thanks. I ordered one myself, but it hasn't come in,"

the kid said, swiping the sweat from his brow and squinting at the chute where a dappled bull waited.

"Get yourself set quickly. Some of these young bulls aren't as accustomed to the chute so they can get impatient. Make sure the rope isn't too close to the front legs. Don't want to cut off oxygen. Hampers the ride and is dangerous for the bull."

"You talking about soaking?"

Cal nodded. "I always play fair with the bulls. I owe them that. And they don't owe me a damn thing but a hard ride. A healthy bull brings a better score if you do your job right."

Wyatt pulled on the helmet and stepped onto the lower slat of the chute.

Hal Sawyer moseyed over. "You ready, kid?"

"Yes, sir, Mr. Sawyer. I was born ready, born to do this like Cal was." Wyatt grinned, looking somehow younger in the bull rider protective gear. His borrowed chaps flapped around his thin legs the same way they had when he was a kid playing cowboy in the front yard.

Cal didn't miss the flicker of doubt in his old friend's eyes. "Let's see it, then."

Wyatt scrambled up and hoisted himself over the fence. Cal couldn't see an ounce of fear in the kid, which was both admirable and scary. Cal leaned over and helped get the rope adjusted around the girth of the bull, double-checking the position, shaking the bell down.

Cal's stomach contracted with nerves as his brother stepped over the back of the bull that bumped against the chute. Wyatt slid the loop down under the belly just as Cal had showed him, cinching the rope tight so the rosined part sat in the correct spot. Then the kid tied the rope off like a pro. The bull didn't like the tightening and twisted its head. Cal wanted to reach over and pluck the kid out, refusing to let him ever climb back in the chute again. But he knew that wouldn't work.

He helped Wyatt position his hand, pressing at his abs. "Get the posture right, Wy. Chest up. When he dips low, use your legs."

Sawyer nodded to the ranch hand standing in the small dirt arena, making sure he was ready to swoop in and distract the bull when the rider came off.

"You call it, kid," Sawyer said, tugging his stained ball cap down and signaling the ranch hand managing the gate.

Wyatt looked at Cal, his brown eyes filled with excitement, with something Cal recognized—determination. The kid nodded. "Cal taught me good. I'm ready."

The ranch hand released the gate and the bull did what it was supposed to do—exploded into the arena, jerking Wyatt. The kid's hand went up but came quickly back down as the bull kicked its back legs. The bull arched into the air, clearing a good foot of air beneath him. Roaring back to earth, the bull spun 180 degrees. Wyatt bounced around like a crash-test dummy, arm flailing, legs flying. A second later his brother went flying over the head of the two-year-old beast. Wyatt hit the ground and then scrambled to get out of the way as the bull turned, head down, coming for him.

"Move, kid," Sawyer muttered under his breath.

Cal felt sour acid rush into his throat. His legs felt like jelly. He'd watched hundreds of guys get tossed in the arena, but he'd never been related to any of them. He'd seen horns puncture sides and hooves sinking into muscle and never felt one bit sickened. But this was his kid brother. Fear pressed against him, squeezing him in its vise grip.

"Goddamn it," Cal yelled, scrabbling over the fence. "I'm coming."

Sawyer caught hold of his leg. "The boys have it, Cal."

Cal paused as Wyatt hightailed it, boots churning up the dust. One of the ranch hands pulled the bull's attention away and the bull turned, lowered his head and bore down on Wyatt's savior who spun expertly out of the way. The escape gate bounced against the metal enclosure and the bull headed toward it, the promise of hay waiting.

Wyatt ran for the fence, scrambling over almost directly opposite where Cal and Sawyer stood. The boy's straw hat sat smashed in the center of the arena, the only casualty on the ride.

"Jesus," Cal sighed, slinking off the top of the fence with relief. He'd never felt so hopeless as he watched the kid hit the dust and have the bull turn on him. Cal wanted to be nonchalant, like he knew this was part of the sport and the toss-off was run-of-the-mill. But for some reason it didn't feel that way.

Hal Sawyer let out a rusty laugh. "Different when it's your kid. Aw, I know he ain't yours, but it's the same concept. Probably have to clean his shorts, but he's fine."

"Right," Cal said as he headed toward Wyatt. Rounding the corner he saw the kid grinning and his heart sank. The kid hadn't been rattled in the least.

"Woo," Wyatt said, running a hand through sweat-soaked hair. "That was crazy, man."

Cal nodded, unable to find his words. He wanted to lecture him but also wanted to praise him for having the balls to ride. What route should he take? He'd been so sure riding a bull would scare the shit out of his little brother that he hadn't planned on something to say when the kid beamed up at him happy as a pig in sunshine after the two-second ride.

Sawyer came on his heels. "Good ride, kid."

"Thank you, Mr. Sawyer. Scared the hell outta me, but I loved it. It's like a rush I've never felt before." Wyatt dusted himself off and grinned at Cal. "Now I know why you do it."

And Cal could see Wyatt did understand the euphoria, the challenge, the need to win. Ruth Whitehorse was going to kill her oldest son. "Yeah."

Wyatt slapped Cal on the back. "We could be a family dynasty, right?"

Cal was silent, managing a nod.

Sawyer grunted, eyeing Wyatt. "How tall are you, son?"

Wyatt's grin flickered. "Uh, I'm nearly six foot."

"And not through growing," Sawyer noted, his expression growing serious. The older man knew Cal's concerns, though Cal had not come out and asked the old cowboy to pop Wyatt's bubble. Something hot flashed across Cal's gut because he knew the man was going to do what he could not. "I'm not sure you've looked around PBR and the PRCA, but most bull riders are squirts. No offense, Cal."

"None taken," Cal said.

"Ain't many six-foot riders and most of them started riding when they were little things. I ain't saying you couldn't do it. You got guts, but you have some things stacked against you. It's a hard life—ask Cal."

Wyatt looked over at him. "I thought you liked being

a bull rider. All those girls, all that money, being on the road. You've always made it sound pretty damn good."

Cal nodded. He *had* always made his life sound good. He figured it helped his mama to know he wasn't lonely or missing her bad cooking. He'd never wanted her to know how crappy he felt nursing a concussion alone in a hotel room or scrabbling to find a few dollars so he could wash his clothes in the laundry mat. So he embellished. "I don't have regrets. But it's rough sometimes. Lonely."

"So?" Wyatt shrugged, walking toward the equipment shed that cast a fat line of shade onto the dusty ground.

Sawyer turned to Cal. "I got the boys pulling Sunny D. He's the grandson of Disastrous D and he'll give you all you want."

"Ranker the bull the better. I haven't ridden in months and need the best you got," Cal said with a smile. He didn't feel like smiling, of course. He felt like a man awaiting execution for some reason. Which was insane. He'd never feared a bull. Whichever one he drew, he rode. No complaints. No qualms. Just a healthy dose of respect for the power of the beast and the damage it could do.

But today he felt different.

Because he knew he wasn't even close to 100 percent. In the past he'd ridden with a bum knee or a few stitches in the side of his head. He'd ridden with a cracked rib, wrists banged and bruised, and once he'd ridden with a cast on his forearm. But the shoulder felt different— sharp pain that took his breath at times and limited range.

The ride would hurt. No doubt about it.

Fifteen minutes later, he tightened his rope and fit his gloved hand beneath the loop, gripping the freshly rosined tail, staring at the curved horns of the massive beast beneath him. The bells on the side of the bull quivered, much like Cal's gut.

"Get him off the gate," Sawyer cautioned as Cal settled his boots against the flanks.

"Got him," Cal said, giving a nod.

The gate pulled and Sunny D shot out, a cannon unloading into the dusty Texas afternoon. The bull bucked hard, leaping, twisting. Cal hung on, allowing his body to anticipate the bull with a naturalness that came to him. He'd done this a thousand times before. Hold on, move. An airhorn sounded. Cal gave a perfect dismount, rolling into the dirt, springing up to look for Sunny D bearing down on him. Instead the bull trotted toward the exit.

Scene. Roll tape. Action. Cut. Couldn't have been scripted any better.

"Hell, yeah!" Wyatt gave a fist pump. Sawyer and his ranch hands wore grins. Cal felt as though he could vomit. The pain was bad, the adrenaline soaked him with sweat that had nothing to do with the hot sun bearing down on them. His legs wobbled as he managed to jog to the perimeter and pull himself onto the fence near where everyone looked on.

"You looked good," Sawyer observed, clasping his hands together. "Not top form, but Sunny D looked atypically sluggish. How's the shoulder?"

Hurt like hell. "Little stiff but good."

Wyatt slapped him on the back. "Man, you rode that son of a gun like a mofo."

"That's just one bull."

"Still," Wyatt said, looking at the crushed cowboy hat in his hand. Cal's gaze stuck on the ripped fibers, bashed and dirty from the bull's hooves. Was that how he'd looked after Rasputin had gotten through with him?

No. He was Cal Lincoln, two-time world champion, a top money earner and resilient cowboy who covered bulls. He wasn't damaged goods. He could live with the pain. Not like he hadn't done it before.

"Thanks, Sawyer, for letting us grab a ride today."

"My pleasure, though I have to admit I wish my bull would have performed better, but I like having riders on my stock. Anytime, fellas."

"Let's go back to Coyote Creek, Wy."

A week passed. Then another. Maggie worked on the house. Charlie, Wyatt and Cal helped her. Floors got refinished, and she painted the exterior a fresh white and added crisp navy shutters. Window boxes were filled with heat-tolerant coreopsis that spilled out, and roses gave a color splash to the whitewashed fence. Cal erected the American flag off the shady porch with its new rocking chairs and porch swing. The Triple J had gone from looking like a crack house to looking like it could grace the cover of *Country Living*.

The box with Bud's ashes in it stared down at her from the top of the pantry like a gynecologist's appointment circled on her calendar. Maggie eyed it several times a day, wondering when she'd get up the nerve to do what she'd promised. It sat waiting, reminded her time slipped away. Soon she'd sign papers on the sale of the house and bid her bull rider adios.

The thought made her heart ache.

But what could she do?

The closer the date Cal would leave got, the more strained their relationship had grown. They'd not even made love last night. After a dinner of nachos in front of the TV, she'd fallen asleep. She could blame it on the new plush couch or the fact she'd been exhausted from spending the day working in the flower beds. Cal had woken her and she'd shuffled off to bed. When she'd awoke that morning, she discovered he hadn't slept with her last night. She'd been alone.

For a moment, lying in the soft dawn light, she'd experienced a loss so severe she couldn't breathe. Her hand moved over the pillow on the left side of the bed— the side he'd chosen for the past month without even asking—and her heart broke apart.

The agreement for a "mutually beneficial, no strings attached" relationship had backfired on her. Because even though they would end as planned, it wasn't going to be painless. No "all the fun, none of the heartache" Cal had promised. She hadn't gotten fat by indulging in a frolic with Cal, but she'd gotten hooked. Her cowboy was a drug. And come Monday—a mere five days away—she'd start rehab. A hard time lay ahead.

Compounding the loss of Cal would be the loss of the Triple J. Though she'd tried to keep perspective, she'd grown to love the place. Bud had been right. It was the sort of place a person found himself or herself. The grasses blowing in the hot wind, the lazy spin of the windmill on the neighboring ranch and the sight of a horse, old as she was, trotting in the early morning dawn was salve to any soul. She'd miss Wyatt with his sleepy morning hair sticking up and the cows that trudged over the hill each evening, coming in for their feed and fresh water. Heck, she'd even miss the irascible Charlie with his weird truck and taciturn manner. And the kitty girl she'd named Tussy after the little witch scratched her. The kittens hadn't even been born yet. What if Maggie never got to see the wee things?

Five days.

"Maggie," Cal called from the front porch.

She set her iPad down. "What?"

"Mom's here to see the house," he called back.

Maggie leaped up and started clearing away the dishes left out at breakfast. Cal had stomped in for coffee around seven o'clock and left the creamer out. Papers she'd used yesterday to line the floor while she chalk-painted the cabinet in the guest bath sat in a jumble. But then she paused at the absurdity. At that moment she'd reacted like a daughter-in-law might have acted. Like she was part of a regular family.

But they weren't a family. She didn't even rank as girlfriend. Hell, technically she was Cal's boss. She sat the cereal bowl down with a clunk.

Pushing out the swinging door, she donned a smile. "Hello."

The older woman turned. "I can't believe how incredible this place looks. You two ought to take this act on the road."

"In another lifetime," Cal said gruffly, looking hot and tired. He, Wyatt and Charlie were painting the pens. A real estate appraiser would be out soon to do a valuation so Maggie could give Hunt Turner a number. He'd already sent an inspector who'd suggested some conditions. One was the state of the pens. That had pissed Cal off and sent him on a mission to make the pens pristine. "I'm out. I'll talk to you later, Mom."

"It's me and you," Ruth said to Maggie, taking her elbow. Maggie had met Ruth only briefly one day when they stopped to pick up Cal's mail. The woman treated her like an old friend.

Ruth's effusive praise warmed Maggie as she escorted

her around the completed rooms. Ruth specifically oohed over the kitchen, not seemingly bothered by the mess left on the counters. "This range is gorgeous. Not that I cook all that much." Ruth ran a hand over the stainless steel.

"I love to cook, but when you're a party of one, take-out is easier," Maggie said.

Ruth grew thoughtful. "Maggie, what are your thoughts about Cal's shoulder?"

Uh-oh.

"He's doing well," she said neutrally.

"Has he talked to you about it?" Ruth pressed.

"Not really. He told me there was a tear that needed repairing, but he's been training and doesn't seem to be having issues." There. That was the truth. No need to mention he often woke at night in obvious pain…or that she'd discovered a new prescription for pain pills…or that Cal grew thunderous when anyone mentioned any concern with his shoulder. He'd nearly taken Charlie's head off for asking how it felt yesterday. She wasn't going to tattle to his mommy.

"Hmm," Ruth said, drumming her polished finger-tips on the new granite. "His surgeon is more than con-cerned. He doesn't feel like his shoulder can hold up. I had hoped I might talk you into bringing it up. Per-haps, probing a bit to see if he might consider having the surgery."

"Why me?"

"Because he cares for and respects you. I can tell. He's never had a woman in his life he trusted other than me and he doubts my motivations. But he trusts you." Ruth walked toward Maggie and placed a hand on her arm, squeezing. "Please. He's so stubborn. I don't want him to end up crippled or disabled or dead because of stubborn pride."

"I don't, either, but I don't have the right to manipulate him that way."

"Oh, not manipulation. Just out-and-out telling him he's a fool." Ruth sounded as though she teased her, but her eyes, ones so similar to Cal's, were rock steady. The woman actually intended Maggie to work on Cal and get him to follow doctor's orders.

"I can't do that, Mrs. Whitehorse."

"Ruth," she said, dropping her hand. "And why not? Don't you love him? Or at least care about him? You don't understand bull riders. They get on those bulls when they can't even see straight. Some of them die because they don't have the sense God gave a billy goat."

Fear curled in Maggie's stomach. Again the vision of Cal crumpled in the dirt, a drooling bull scooping him up and tossing him into the air, bloomed in her head. Would Cal riding with an injured shoulder lead him to misjudge things during the ride? Would his balance be off? Would the pain cloud his decision-making in the arena? Maggie didn't know. She didn't know anything about the sport of bull riding other than it was dangerous and required a cocksure, experienced cowboy. "I understand your fears, but *you* should talk to him. You're his family."

"I have. He gets angry, lies to me about the pain. He's always been unreasonable, and you seem such a reasonable girl. Like you could talk a snowman into buying ice cubes."

"I can't do that."

"Just a little talk about making wise decisions. It could make a difference."

Maggie knew she couldn't convince the woman she had no sway over her son so she nodded. "I can try."

"Oh, good. I've been so worried about him. You know, he's headstrong like his father. Whatever Dave wanted he was going to get and to hell with everyone else. But Cal's been different these last weeks. He seems more at peace. More comfortable around me and Wyatt. He's never realized how much he's belonged here. I guess I don't want him to end up like his father, always searching, never thinking about others. He needs a home, a place he feels safe. I think he feels that way here with you."

"You know I'm selling this place, right? That I'm going back home?"

Ruth stepped back. It was obvious she thought differently. "But what about Cal? I thought you two were—"

"We're not what you think we are, Ruth."

"I have eyes. You two are in love." Ruth looked at Maggie like she was an idiot for not seeing something so obvious. But what Ruth saw was her son in a relationship. Of course the relationship was as temporary as the tattoos Maggie used to slap on her arm each summer, but Ruth didn't know that. She saw what she wanted to see.

Maggie sighed. "Ruth, Cal's going to ride in the next BFT series, whatever that is, and I don't have the authority or power to change that. I'll try to talk to him about his family's concerns, but don't hold out hope. After all, Cal is a grown man who knows himself better than anyone. If he says he can ride, he will."

Ruth looked as if Maggie had kicked her dog. "No. He doesn't know his limitations. He's a rodeo man and that means he'd rather kill himself than do as instructed. I thought you could help. It was a last-ditch effort to get my son to take care of himself, to think about those who love him for once."

"I'm sorry. If it's any consolation, I think he'll do fine. He's determined and he's been going to therapy and working hard to get stronger."

"Of course," Ruth said, inhaling and then releasing a huge sigh. "It's not just his shoulder, though. It's the two serious concussions, the worn-out cartilage in his knees and the broken ankle that didn't heal right. I don't know how much more his body can take. How much more I can take of watching my son tossed around like a rag doll."

Maggie didn't have the words. What could she say to this woman who wanted her son to quit rodeo?

For a few moments they stood in silence.

Finally, Ruth slapped her hands together. "Let's go see the barn."

"Okay," Maggie said, opening the back door. She wanted to shut Ruth out and lock it. She wanted to run to Cal and shake him and scream for him to stop riding bulls…to give up the sport…to stay in Texas…to spend every night beside her because she lov—

No.

She couldn't, wouldn't, shouldn't love Cal "Hollywood" Lincoln.

They walked out the door and found Cal hooking his trailer to his truck.

15

CAL WAS SO angry he could spit. So he did. Right into the dirt next to his trailer hitch.

So Maggie and his mom were conspiring to keep him sidelined, to use the feelings he had for both of them to manipulate him?

The thought pissed him off so bad he couldn't think of anything else but getting the hell away from them. From everyone. Hell, that was probably why his dad had left. Every man knew it was a fact women hid their true motivations behind good intentions. *I'm so worried about you. I just want you safe. Use common sense. You're going to kill yourself. Hand me your balls so I can put them on the shelf.*

It wasn't about *their* fears. It was about bringing a man to heel.

He'd been working on the pens when he remembered he'd told Wyatt he'd send him a pair of old spurs. The kid still wanted to ride. Cal had failed to dissuade the kid, but he'd already discussed all of this with his mom. He reminded her of Wyatt's propensity for picking up new hobbies that he obsessed over for a few months before setting them aside for something new and shiny. His mother agreed she'd wait rodeo out the same way she'd done with karate, lacrosse and countless other activities. When Cal had come up the back kitchen steps and opened the door he heard his mother pleading with Maggie to talk to him, to use the trust and affection he had for her to manipulate him.

And did Maggie say no?

No.

She said she'd try.

His heart had withered in his chest as the sour taste of betrayal coated his mouth. He stepped off the stoop, not drawing any attention to himself, stunned the woman he'd spent the past month loving and laughing with could even think about conspiring with someone to take away the only thing he cared about. How could she do something like that to him? Hadn't he opened himself to her, telling her about what his mother and Charlie had done in the past? Hadn't he told her how much his mother nagged him about quitting, about doing something less dangerous? Didn't Maggie know how much his career meant to him…how much coming back after the injury meant to him?

And she agreed to talk him out of it?

The door opened and both the women stepped out, shading their eyes with their hands. He didn't say anything. Just kept working on hooking the trailer to the back of his pickup truck.

"What are you doing?" Maggie asked, moving toward him.

"Hooking up the trailer."

"I can see that, but why?" She stopped beside him and he could smell the lavender lotion she'd smoothed over her legs when she'd gotten out of the shower earlier that day. He'd told her he loved the scent of lavender... that it made him horny. She'd put it all over her body. Cal had swept her into his arms, tossed her on the bed and made love to her just to prove how serious he was. Now the scent rubbed his face in the betrayal.

"Because I'm leaving early."

"You're leaving early?" Maggie repeated, stepping back as he brushed by her. "What's wrong? I don't understand. The pens aren't finished and you said you weren't leaving until Wednesday."

"I changed my mind," he said tersely. It would be better this way, anyway. No more dreading Wednesday, no more making love to her and growing almost weepy at the thought of leaving her. Rip the bandage off and forget about it. Done. Over. *Finito.*

"Why? We were going to go to that steak house in McKinney. Wait, what's wrong? You're acting crazy." She tried to put her hand on his arm, but he shrugged it off. Half of him wanted to stop and talk things out. Tell her she couldn't control him that way. Tell her using his feelings against him was so wrong. But what would it matter? They were over in a few days, anyway. And he didn't want to talk about his goddamned feelings. He wanted to ride. Conquer. Prove he was worthy in this world.

"I'm fine. Just realizing I need to get to Mobile early. Clear my head."

"I don't understand," she said, her voice full of tears. That sound tore at his resolve, pecked at his heart, but he wouldn't be tricked. He wouldn't be moved by her tears or anything else. He was a man resolved.

"I do," Ruth said, setting her hands on her hips. "You're running. Just like your—"

"You know, Mom, I'm not like him. You don't have a right to say something like that. What happened between my father and you is your hang-up. You've used it as a crutch your whole life and you've allowed it to shape our relationship. You need therapy and you need to stop trying to control me, Wyatt and Gary. No one's leaving you. No one thinks you're not important. My dad was a shitty man who hurt you. That's been over for a long time so let it go. Just let it go."

"You heard," Ruth said, her features shifting into the face she'd used when he'd refused his peas or knocked a glass of iced tea onto the floor.

He stared flatly at both of the women he loved and set the cowboy hat he'd left on the bumper on his head. "I'm going to Mobile. I have a career and a life to live. No one is going to force me to live her vision of it. I choose to be a cowboy. I choose the life I've always had because that's who I am."

Maggie grabbed his arm. "You think I'd try to stop you?"

He pulled away. "Honey, I heard what you said. You'd try to talk to me, try to make me see reason. I know what kind of woman you are. You live safe. I don't." With that, he turned and strode to his truck. He'd left his toiletries and his favorite pair of jeans inside the Triple J, but he wasn't stopping. He had to get away before he did and said something he'd really regret.

He needed space.

Wide-open space.

He'd drop the trailer at Charlie's place, drive to Mobile and get his mind right. He had a ride waiting on him there. He had a name to uphold, a career to resurrect.

Firing the engine, he put the truck in Reverse, watching Maggie and his mother move back so they wouldn't get run over. He felt like an ass, but even more than that, he felt deep, utter anguish.

Maggie didn't understand him, after all.

RAIN HAD COME that afternoon and washed away some of the heat and dust. For once it felt decent outside. Not cool. But decent. Like sweat didn't roll down her back and her shorts didn't stick to her thighs. The evening came soft like an apology.

Maggie stood in the far pasture, watching the grass sway against the paintbrush sky spread out before her. Tears streaked her cheeks, half of them over the stubborn, dumb-ass cowboy who'd driven away a few days ago and half for the loss she held in her hands. Bud had elected to get a simple urn for his ashes. Ever the pragmatist in things such as this, his romantic nature was captured only by the place he'd requested his ashes be spread.

His children hadn't wanted to do it and when the ranch was left to the girl who "thought she was somebody," Julian had delivered the ashes to her and told her she could deposit the ashes since she was the one who now owned the place.

He'd said *deposited*. Like it was no big deal.

She looked down at the urn. "Well, I did what you wanted. I brought you back to the place you loved. Even fixed it the way you would have expected me to."

Pulling the lid off the urn, she said, "Here you go, Bud. Be at peace."

She tipped the urn, making sure the wind was to her back and carefully began emptying the contents. As she walked along the hard Texas terrain, she said a prayer for the man who'd been such a part of her life. There was a sense of rightness in her actions, even as the tears dripped off her jaw, landing on her T-shirt. Perhaps she should have worn something nicer than shorts and a T, but Bud would have scoffed. Too hot to be uncomfortable.

"Goodbye, Bud." She set the lid back onto the urn, wondering what she was supposed to do with the thing now. What were the rules for a used urn?

She carefully stepped through the grass and walked back to the rental car. She should have worn her cowboy boots, but hadn't bothered with being practical. She'd been sitting at the kitchen table, crying into her sweet tea when she'd seen the box in the pantry. The signed offer sent over by Hunt Turner sat on the counter. The man had given her a fair price, more than she'd expected. With a heavy heart, she'd scrawled her signature on each marked blank. The Triple J would belong to someone else and she'd go back east and figure out her life. And with that grim thought, she had gotten up, grabbed the box with Bud's ashes and driven to the back pasture. As if a demon was on her heels, she felt the need to complete her original task.

She opened the box to set the urn inside and spied a letter she'd not seen earlier.

On the outside was scrawled *Margaret Anne Stanton* in Bud's handwriting. Maggie lifted the envelope, set the urn in the box and climbed onto the back of the car, wincing at the heat of the trunk.

"Damn Texas heat," she muttered, ripping the seal and pulling out a handwritten note on Bud's personal stationery.

Dear Maggie,

I'm sure you're wondering how I knew you'd be the person disposing of my ashes. Rest assured I know what value I was in the eyes of my children. I felt confident you'd see my wishes carried out. You always do.

It has also occurred to me you might question why I would leave you a place so far from where you call home. Suffice it to say, I had a hunch. As a child you lounged on the couch in my office, staring at the photos I'd taken at the Triple J and eagerly sat, eyes wide, when I told you stories of my time at the ranch. You were the only person who listened to my tales with any interest.

As you grew into a smart, lovely young woman, I began to imagine you more my daughter than the housekeeper's girl or the assistant who filed my contracts. A shrink could probably make much of that, but it comforted me to think of you that way. I had not ruined you by giving you too much or loving you not enough, and you pleased me with your tenacity, adaptability and loyalty. I wanted to give you something I thought would be perfect for the dreamer beneath the business suit. In you, I saw myself.

So I leave you the only place I felt myself. Your first inclination will be to sell the place. But I am betting if you spend any time there, you will find a place to belong. You've enough grit, smarts and sass to pull it off, Maggie. Don't be afraid to be less than practical. When you follow your heart rather than your head, you end up with a life fulfilled rather than one merely lived. Thank you for caring for me, dear girl. You have been a delight and deserve only the best. That's why I left you a piece of Texas.

With love and appreciation,

Bud

THE WORDS BLURRED as a sob ripped through her. Guilt mixed in with her grief as she thought about those papers she'd signed a mere hour before. Bud had loved her enough to give her a future he thought she deserved and she'd let it go. Why? Because she thought it sensible. And it was.

She'd convinced herself she didn't belong here. But maybe she did. Where someone belonged was up to them, right? Just because it made sense to go back home and rely on her skills to create a life didn't mean she *had* to. After all, the past few weeks she'd spent in Texas hadn't been good just because she'd fallen in love with a cowboy. No. She'd fallen in love with the Triple J. With the sad horse and the freshly painted porch. With the way the sun fell through the windows onto the warm wood floors…and that soaker tub had her name written all over it. The cat had given birth to kittens in the barn yesterday. Five scrawny, mewling kitties who rooted for milk. The feral cat had even allowed Maggie to pick up one kitten. Wasn't that a sign? Even the barn cat thought she belonged.

Because deep down underneath her sensibility she longed to keep the Triple J.

She longed to be at home…finally.

Bud had given her a fresh start. The Triple J was that fresh start and it belonged to her.

Two minutes later she bumped to a halt beside the pretty white farmhouse. She climbed out and gave a wave to Charlie who had just fed Sissy. Maggie had caught him cooing to the kittens earlier. The man hadn't smelled like bourbon in over a week. He looked better as each day passed. More alive.

Maggie looked over at the house, the earlier grief slinking away, the heartache softening just a bit. It looked like home. Because it was home.

Cal had hurt her when he'd thrown ugly accusations at her. She'd not had a chance to defend herself against his words. He'd left, like a little boy taking his toys away. Maggie had known he had an issue with people he loved meddling in his life. But she hadn't been doing that no matter what he thought he'd overheard. His leaving had hurt and she'd spent the entirety of two nights in bed, crying over the injury done to her heart.

She'd cried this morning, too, when she'd awoken alone.

When she'd drunk her hot tea alone.

When she'd accepted the real estate contract delivered by courier.

But now she knew she could heal. She loved Cal, but she wouldn't allow him to break her and send her running back to Philly.

Her cowboy boots sat beside the front door she'd painted teal blue. Like a symbol of her future. Like they were waiting for her to claim who she was.

Maggie kicked her flip-flops off and slid her feet into her boots.

Then she went inside the house to tear up the real estate contract.

16

CAL HADN'T EVEN made it to the Louisiana border before he knew he'd been a jackass. And by the time he crossed into Mississippi, he felt like turning around.

But he didn't.

Because he was a man and there was this thing inside every man called pride. And pride liked to toss out comments like "don't be such a pussy" or "you don't need that shit" or "plenty of fish in the sea." Pride was the trash-talker, the destroyer of romance and the chief instigator of divorce, job loss and world wars. Pride needed its ass whipped, but Cal wouldn't do it because it all felt too raw.

So he kept driving, stopping for an occasional Red Bull or a can of Skoal in order to push through to Mobile. He arrived in the middle of the night, exhausted, haunted by his behavior and wired on too much caffeine. No bars were open, so he grabbed a motel on the outskirts of town and bought a six-pack at an all-night convenience store where a prostitute asked him if he wanted some company.

No. Company was the last thing on his mind.

He went back to his room, drank three beers, showered, dried off with a stiff towel that smelled like bleach and collapsed onto the squeaky bed. When he woke up, it was one o'clock in the afternoon and his head felt like a ripe melon waiting to split open.

A drive by the arena proved useless. It was as dead as a cemetery but with fewer flowers. So Cal checked out of his room, drove down to the Gulf coast and got a hotel room at a casino. For the next few days he gambled a little, walked the beach and religiously performed the stretches the physical therapist had given him to do daily. He also stared at his phone, praying Maggie would call.

But, of course, she wouldn't. And didn't.

Why would she? He'd acted like an immature asshole. Accusing her of meddling in his life, storming off like a little kid. The whole episode embarrassed him, but at the moment he'd been so incensed. Anger and hurt rampaged through his body, making him like the bulls he rode—irrational, dangerous and too stupid to know he overreacted. He'd been terribly wrong to leave that way. He'd told her it would be a clean break, no hard feelings, no leaving her hanging with the ranch. But he'd not upheld his end of the deal.

Had he hurt her?

He knew he had. He'd seen it in her eyes when he'd lashed out.

So why didn't he fix it? Call her, tell her he was an idiot, beg her to come to Mobile...or stay in Texas. Forever.

But he knew the answer. He was scared of needing Maggie. Never before had he needed anyone other than himself. His life had been simple—get up, work out, ride bulls. That had always been enough, and he didn't want that to change. Cal didn't need that sort of weakness in his life. Love made a man soft and cowboys weren't soft. They cowboyed up and rode hurt, so how much different was a busted heart from a busted leg?

Cal would bear it.

And as he kicked at the last wave on the white beach he vowed to do just that. Suck it up, forget about Maggie and ride. His goal hadn't changed because he was stupid enough to fall in love. Or whatever it was he felt for Maggie. Eye on the prize waiting on him in Vegas.

Cal packed up his gear and drove back to Mobile.

Two days later, his shoulder hurt like shit, he'd slept like shit and he looked like…shit. Not the best way to feel before facing some of the rankest bulls in any event thus far. The promoter had done a good job lining up the best stock and all the regular guys were in the locker room when Cal strolled in.

"Well, if it ain't ol' Hollywood," Crank Daniels drawled, slapping Cal on the back. He managed not to wince. "You get tired of modelin' and decide to start slummin' again?"

"Shut up, Crank," Cal growled, setting his gear on a bench and unzipping it. "You act like you're a durn redneck and we all know your mama's eating squab and pâté back in River Oaks."

"Shiiit." Crank laughed, plopping his skinny ass onto a chair and pulling out athletic tape to wrap the ankle he'd broken in Laredo.

Antonio Morez cast dark eyes on Cal. "It's good to see you, friend."

Cal managed a smile. "You, too."

Tony was serious and deeply religious, often taking time to meditate before each ride, whereas Crank could sub in for a rodeo clown at a moment's notice. The

number-two-ranked bull rider was as notorious for the
pranks he played on his fellow riders as he was his ability to cover any bull on a given day. Both were talented
riders and decent friends. One to pray with, one to raise
hell with.

"Who'd you draw?" Crank asked.

"Raisin' Cane." Cal felt good about the bull he'd ride
for his first true outing since the surgery. Cane had a
mean streak and hadn't been ridden in his past three out-
ings. Which meant he could bring a good score.

"That's the sort they give old cripples like you, Hollywood," Crank said with a twinkle in his eye.

Cal gave Crank a choice finger and then started getting ready for his comeback.

An hour later, Cal strolled out with his fellow riders to be introduced in the arena. Usually the strobe
lights and the explosions amped him. He loved the roar
of the crowd and the almost obnoxious behavior of the
announcer—it was all part of the experience. But tonight
he felt hollow. Nothing had changed, so he didn't know
why it all felt like a letdown. When had strapping up to
ride the hell out of a bull felt more a job than a thrill?

And the cold sweat dripping down his back didn't
help.

He wasn't scared.

He was fearless.

All he needed was to hang on for eight seconds and
grab a good score.

Three hours later he walked out of the stadium,
smiled and signed autographs and accepted congratu-
lations from the fans who'd waited in the light drizzle to
take a picture with him. His shoulder hurt like hell, but
the adrenaline still coursing through his body took the

edge off. Cal should have been ecstatic, but he couldn't get there. His comeback ride had been anticlimactic.

And that sucked.

As he waved good-night to his fellow competitors, he reached for his phone. No messages. Not from his mother. Or his brother. Or the woman he'd left in Texas wounded by his dumbassery.

"Hey, Cal, come with us," Crank called across the parking lot. "We're heading to the Rocking C for beer and women."

Any other night and Cal might have joined Crank and some of the other rowdier bull riders, but he didn't have the heart for it. He wouldn't mind a beer but the noise and the chicks tipping drunkenly into his lap were so far off his menu at the moment, he might as well be in another restaurant. "Another time."

"Your loss, man. These Bama chicks are smokin'," Crank said, parking his hat on his amber locks and grinning like a fool at the two blondes walking beside him. They gave the requisite giggle.

Cal didn't respond. Just climbed into his truck and fired the engine. Taking two pain pills from the bottle in his pocket, he popped them, swigging tepid water from the half-filled bottle in his cup holder. Then he headed back to his lonely motel room. Once there, he pulled off his boots and lay on the bed, trying not to cry.

Seriously.

Tears crept into his eyes as he tried to focus on the cheap light cover and not on the ache in his shoulder. Or the ache in his heart.

Never had he felt so alone, so resigned to a life such as this. But it had been the life he'd chosen. Every time a woman got close, he pushed her away. And this time his controlled five-week love affair had backfired like Charlie's truck did every time he pulled out of the Triple J.

"Shit," he said to the room. It, of course, said nothing back because rooms didn't talk. At least not with words. This room, however, could tell the tale of a cowboy such as Cal. It would tell of wanderlust and fast-food dinners. It would share chapters on one-night stands and the hollow promise of a phone call. Chapters on cheap stolen towels, unused Bibles in the nightstand and coverlets that when hit with a blue light would reveal tales of horror.

Who lived this way?

Cowboys like him.

Cal rolled over on his good shoulder, closed his eyes and went to sleep on top of the flowered bedspread still wearing his jeans and pearl-snap Western shirt.

CAL MADE THE finals and he was only one spot out of the big money.

And he'd pulled Rasputin in the final round.

The bull who had landed him in the hospital, under the knife and nearly three months off the tours.

"You drew Razz?" Antonio asked, his husky voice over Cal's right shoulder.

"That's called fate," Crank said before Cal could respond.

"That's one thing I'd call it," Cal said, trying to smile, trying to pretend his life was the same as it always had been. Thing was, what bothered him wasn't his nerves. He'd ridden Sweet Baby Boy last night for an average score. Combined with his ride on Raisin' Cane, he had enough to make the finals. Part of him felt relief at being able to strap on his chaps and jump right back into the arena, but the other half of him felt an emotional distance from the sport he'd always loved.

Maybe he didn't have it anymore.

Not the physical ability. He'd proven that to himself whether he rode Rasputin or not. But it was the desire. Had it withered inside him or had he allowed the lazy lifestyle of eating fried chicken on Sundays at his mama's dinner table paired with making love with Maggie as the sun came up to steal what had always burned so hot inside him?

He didn't know.

But something was wrong with him.

Thirty minutes later he stood near the chute. Rasputin had been loaded and Cal was ready as he'd ever be. The ache in his shoulder was small in comparison to the adrenaline surging through his body. The last time he'd climbed onto Razz, he'd been defeated. Today he'd not leave the same way. Conviction sat inside him.

He climbed into the chute and slid his rope beneath the bull's belly. Razz held still, the consummate professional. Crank helped him secure the rope and position the bells. Cal swung his leg over and settled onto the burly bull's back, cinching the rope tight several times.

At his nod, the chute opened.

Rasputin was as wily a beast as his namesake and the bull knew how to buck a rider off first thing. He spun, bucked hard to the right, kicking up his back legs, catching air. Over and over the bull pounded the earth. Cal stopping thinking and fell into the ride, allowing his body to take over. The bull rocked, rolled and spun. Dirt kicked up, the faces of the cheering crowd nothing but a mottled blur as Cal tightened his legs, digging his spurs to lift himself and ride the monstrosity. Finally, after what seemed like forever the buzzer sounded.

Cal executed an awkward dismount, scrabbling for the nearest fence because he knew the bull had a nasty temper. And sure enough, Rasputin came after him, head low. Cal made it to the fence and pulled himself toward the top. But his shoulder popped and sharp pain shot up his arm. He faltered, his legs churning against the advertisements of sponsors. He felt the bull and heard the bull fighters. One wicked horn grazed his waist, but the fighters were able to distract the bull and guide him toward the exit.

Cal dropped down, breathing hard, clutching his shoulder. No sense in pretending like he didn't hurt. No doubt his small tear was a large tear now. And it had nothing to do with the ride. He'd done it pulling himself out of harm's way.

He spit out his mouthpiece and waited for the score.

His score flashed on the big screen: 89.7.

The crowd erupted into cheers, and Cal waved his cowboy hat, acknowledging them. The score was enough to move into first. With three other riders left, he could drop to second or third, but it was a solid score that might move him up in the overall rankings once the weekend was done.

Cal didn't bother going to see Tubby and have him look at the shoulder. He knew he'd injured it again. Knew there was little to be done for it. He'd pop the pain pills and see how it felt in the morning. Once he reached the locker room, he thumbed the lid off his pills, popped a few and spent some time unwrapping his ankle and icing an old knee injury. He longed for a shower, but didn't want to go back to the motel room alone. And he still had a contractual obligation to sign autographs after the event.

An hour later with a check in his pocket, a sense of accomplishment at having moved up to third in the overall standings, and a manageable ache in his shoulder, Cal walked into the Rocking C Bar and Grill.

The joint was rowdy with a jubilant crowd and two-for-one drink specials for anyone with a PBR ticket. Cal made his way through the crush to the bar, nodding at the people who called out "welcome back" and "nice ride." Finally he pushed in beside Crank who was already two beers up on him.

"Nice job out there, old man," Crank said, with a gleam in his eye. He slapped the bar and a girl in a tight halter top came running. "A Bud Light for my man here, sexy."

The bartender whose name tag read Holly smiled. "Whatever you want, Crank."

"That's music to my ears," Crank said to Cal with a laugh.

"I may be old, but I went three for three, snot-nosed brat," Cal said, taking the ice-cold beer bottle from Holly who wore stars in her eyes for the cocky Crank.

Crank clinked his bottle against Cal's. "Touché."

Cal took a long draw, wishing he'd begged off. He'd wanted to get his mojo back, but all he could think about was what Maggie was doing at the moment. Was she popping corn and settling in to watch Netflix? Or was she watching over the barn cat due to give birth any day now? Or maybe she'd already gone back east.

He wished he was in Coyote Creek with her…or even

New Jersey or wherever else she planned to go once she ditched the Triple J.

"You know what you need?" Crank said, interrupting his thoughts.

Cal eyed the younger cowboy.

"A cowgirl."

Shaking his head, Cal took another swig. "That's the last thing I need."

"No, no. Me? I got tossed. You, however, need to celebrate your comeback. Like right down there is a pretty gal. Long dark hair, kick-ass rack, and she's been watching you since you walked in."

"No, thanks," Cal said.

"But you ain't even looked at her. And she's prime real estate, my friend. I'm going to send her a drink."

"Don't," Cal said.

"You don't want her? Fine. I'll take a crack."

Cal focused on peeling the label from his beer and wondered why he'd agreed to come meet the guys for a drink. He knew what went down after each event. If a guy didn't get in a brawl, he spent all night weeding out which chick he'd take back to his hotel room. That a roommate might be in the next bed didn't matter. Sometimes the after-rodeo party became a Roman orgy.

Not his scene.

Which is why he should take his ass back to the motel, load his truck and head back to Maggie. He missed the hell out of her and maybe this wasn't love…or maybe it was. But either way, he couldn't live like this anymore. He'd kiss her feet, lick her boots or whatever else she deemed appropriate for an idiot like him. He set his half-empty beer on the bar and prepared to leave Mobile and head home.

Home.

He'd called Coyote Creek home before but he'd never felt as if it was truly where he belonged. But now? Yeah. It felt like where he wanted to be.

Please, God, let her still be there.

"Thanks for the drink," someone said behind him. Cal stiffened because her voice sounded so sweet and familiar.

"No problem, hon," Crank said, pulling away from Cal and shifting toward the woman he'd sent the beer to. "I can't stand the sight of a pretty woman sitting by herself. Not very gentlemanly of me to not offer you a drink and some company."

Cal grunted at the lame comment. As if any woman would fall for that.

Then he caught the woman's scent—lavender and sunshine.

She smelled like—he spun around on the stool— Maggie.

"I've found most cowboys to be such gentlemen," Maggie said, taking a sip of the beer Crank had sent her way. She looked right at Cal. "Some not so much."

Cal didn't know whether to kiss her or run for the door.

'Cause she looked mad.

"That's right," Crank said, leaning close and setting a big paw on her waist, pulling her toward him. "And you look like a lady who needs a gentleman tonight."

Cal curled his hand into a fist as Maggie gave Crank a smile. "I do."

"That's enough," Cal said, sliding off the stool and taking Maggie by the arm.

Crank shot Cal a look that said "back off" and Maggie pulled her arm from his grasp.

"What are you doing here?" Cal asked her, ignoring Crank.

"I came to get a cowboy."

17

MAGGIE WANTED TO kiss Cal. She wanted to tell him how relieved and proud she was of him for riding Rasputin to the buzzer. She also wanted to punch him in his big, fat, stupid nose.

Total toss-up.

The young cowboy who'd sent her a cold beer pulled at Cal's arm. "Now see here, Hollywood, you passed. Step on, brother."

Cal's gaze never left hers. "I understand, Crank, but this is a different situation."

"How so?"

"Because the cowboy she wants is me," Cal said with not the slightest trace of arrogance. No need to be. She had come for him.

In a way.

After she'd torn up the contract Hunt Turner had sent, she'd sat down at the kitchen table to think. So often in her life she knew automatically what had to be done, but this time she hadn't a clue. She was keeping the Triple J, but she needed a plan. Without any experience at ranching and with so little acreage, she struck off the idea of raising cattle. The land wasn't necessarily suitable for farming. She didn't think. She knew nothing about farming, anyhow. For a good hour, she'd scratched a few ideas on a legal pad. A dude ranch? But was Coyote Creek too far from a major airport to sustain a successful tourist operation? A bed-and-breakfast? Maybe she could lease it to movie production companies? She'd racked her brain for an idea of how she could actually feed herself and the animals.

But it was Wyatt who'd tossed out the most viable decision when he came to tell her good-night and ask if she'd talked to Cal.

Thing was, in order to do what Wyatt suggested she needed the hardheaded cowboy who'd jumped to conclusions and skipped out on her.

So she'd bought a used truck, locked up the house and driven across the South to get to Mobile. She'd made it in time to watch Cal ride Rasputin. She'd never seen anything like that man ride. Her heart had beaten hard in her ears and she'd felt nausea rise in her throat as he climbed on, but nothing had been more thrilling than watching him hold on to that bull. No, not just hold on. Ride him.

She'd thought to show up in his autograph line but what set between them seemed too personal to air out in front of fans. So she planned to follow his truck back to his hotel like some crazy stalker chick. But he hadn't gone back to the hotel. Instead he'd gone to a bar. Which had hurt her feelings a little. She'd spent several nights crying into her pillow over the jerk and he was going out on the town? She chalked it up to a celebration and climbed out of the new-to-her, only-dinged-on-the-passenger-side-door Chevy truck and went inside to wait on Cal to notice she was there.

Thankfully, after fending off a few too-interested cowboys, Cal's friend had noticed her.

Cal's buddy frowned. "Bull to the shit. She ain't here for no broken-down old fart like you."

Maggie smiled at the kid. "Actually this cowboy still owes me some work."

Crank looked confused.

Cal nodded. "She's my boss."

"What the hell?" Crank asked.

"I'm his boss and he left without finishing some things. So I'm here to bring him back." She looked at Cal when she said it.

The cowboy with the boyish smile and too-long hair shrugged. "Whatever, weirdos." And then he turned back to the bar, knocking his knuckles on the scarred wood.

Cal was absolutely still, studying her as she stood in the middle of the loud, crowded bar, wearing her new jeans with the rhinestone bling on the pockets and the boots they'd bought at the Co-op. "You came to get me?"

"Sorta."

Someone jostled her and she stepped aside so she didn't get trampled. Country music blared and the roar of conversation made it hard for anyone to hear anything. "Wanna go outside?" he asked.

She nodded.

Cal took her arm and wound through the bar, pushing out into the hot, humid Alabama night. A few people loitered in the parking lot, some kissing, some shooting the breeze. Night cloaked them in intimacy. Here's where the road met the rubber…another saying she'd learned from the painters.

They walked to Cal's truck and he lowered the tailgate. Jerking his head, he invited her to sit. She shook her head. No way could she sit when she felt this keyed up.

"First before you say anything I have to apologize," Cal said, leaning against the lip of the tailgate. "I was an asshole. I shouldn't have overreacted or accused you of trying to control me. I know you better than that, and after I thought about it, I knew my mama had cornered you. She's hard to say no to."

Maggie nodded. "Yeah, she is."

"I told her you reminded me of her."

She jerked her head around. "How so?"

"You're hard to say no to," he said with a smile. It was a shamefaced smile, and she could see he was embarrassed about his behavior. He should be.

"You shouldn't have stormed off that way. It was immature and irrational and—"

"Dumb ass," he finished.

"That and not fair to me. You told me it wouldn't end that way."

"I know."

She crossed her arms. "I would never try to stop you from doing what you love. I can see the passion you have for riding. But I also understand how your mother feels. It's a dangerous sport. You have a lot of scars to prove it."

"I'm a regular ol' collector of hurt, ain't I?"

"So you hurt me?" She didn't want the emotion to fall into her voice, but she was helpless to stop it.

"I didn't want either one of us to hurt. This thing between us was supposed to be simple. Have fun and part with a smile on our faces, but it didn't work that way. I went off in a huff, but then I missed the hell out of you. Kept thinking about things I wanted to show you, like the dolphins I saw in the Gulf or the way the sun set over the water. But I had shoved you away with my insecurities. I was afraid of my feelings, and like a selfish, immature kid I ran away from the hard stuff."

"I don't want to be your hard stuff," she said, wondering what he meant. Why was she the hard stuff?

"You aren't." He looked out at the trucks. Seconds ticked by. "Why did you really come? Not just to hear an apology?"

"No, I wanted to propose something to you."

"Propose?"

"A partnership. I didn't sell the Triple J."

He jerked his gaze to her. "Why not?"

"Because I didn't want to let it go. Bud left me a note. He challenged me to not think with my head but to follow my gut. Somehow, that made sense. I refused Hunt Turner's offer and I'm staying in Texas."

"You're staying?" Cal's voice held something that sounded like hope and that gave her the needed courage to ask him a pretty big thing.

"Yes, and I am hoping you'll lend me your name."

"Like get married?" He sounded even more shocked than when she'd told him she hadn't sold the ranch.

Maggie's heart jolted at the words *get married*. "No. Like in a business partnership. I want to make the Triple J into a ranch that provides stock for rodeos. I've been reading a lot of information about stock contractors. Your brother actually gave me the idea. The Triple J is the perfect size and we've already got a good-size barn. I've sketched out—"

"Wait, you're staying in Texas and you want to raise

bulls?" Cal sounded shocked again. She thought shocking him might be a good side hobby. He made some funny faces when surprised.

"Yes, that's what I'm telling you. I've worked on a business plan and I think I can get a loan that will float us until we can get some more cows and buy some straws of bull sperm. Proven bulls have expensive sperm. Until we can become viable stock contractors, we can sell some older cattle for beef and even run a training facility for bull riders or provide boarding for horses or something. I'm not exactly clear on what opportunities might come our way, or my way rather, but I know this is something I can do. I have a good acumen for business and a can-do attitude for a city slicker."

Cal started laughing. "What do you need me for?"

"The sperm."

"The sperm?"

"Are you going to keep repeating everything I say?" she said, crossing her arms and glaring at him. "I need your connections and your name. This is still a good-ol'-boys network and you're a top-notch bull rider. You have an 'in' I don't have. So I'm offering you a partnership."

"A business partnership?"

Maggie huffed. "Jesus, Joseph and Mary, do you need to clean out your ears? Yes, a business arrangement."

"No."

Maggie's heart sank. "But why not? It would be a good investment."

"I'm not saying it wouldn't be, but I'm not interested in just a business relationship with you, Mags."

"What are you interested in?"

"A forever sort of relationship." Cal caught her at her waist and pulled her to him.

"You're talking about…?"

"Me, you and a barn cat named…Sue?"

"I named her Tuss," Maggie said, clamping her hands on his forearms and pushing against him. "And I'm not sure we're ready for that sort of commitment."

"Stop thinking with your head, Maggie. Think with your heart," he said, dragging her to him. He set his forehead against hers and looked deep into her eyes. "Bud was right. Go with your gut. Mine tells me you are the woman I've been waiting for. I didn't even know it, but you are exactly what this cowboy needs."

"But—"

His lips caught her protest. She allowed the logic to fade into the background and she slipped into a rightness that existed only in Cal's arms. He gathered her to him, growing bolder. His tongue slipped inside her mouth and he groaned, breaking the kiss to say, "Oh, Mags, I missed you so much, baby. I'm so sorry. Please say you'll forgive me. Say you'll stay with me."

Maggie pulled back. "But what does that mean?"

"It means I want to live with you at the Triple J. I want to raise bulls with you, teach young guys how to ride and make love to you every night. I want to be your business partner, your life partner, your sun and moon."

"You want to live with me?" she repeated, her heart once again thudding in her ears.

"And love with you. Somehow I've fallen for you. I've been so miserable these last few days trying to get my old life back. I couldn't. Know why?"

She looked up at him.

"Because you changed me. I'm not the man I was. I'm a new one. One with a future."

"Are you sure?" she asked, staring at him. She wanted

him to mean it. More than anything she wanted to start this new life with Cal beside her.

A fresh start together.

"More than I'm sure of anything. I don't know how much longer I'll ride. May be done this year, but I want a future to look forward to. I want a future with you."

Maggie smiled. "You love me?"

"I do," he said, giving her another kiss.

Lifting up on her toes, Maggie kissed him. "I love you, too, cowboy."

"Don't make it too easy on me now," he said with a grin.

Maggie studied that face she loved so much, marveling over how everything had changed in a matter of minutes. Cal loved her. She'd gone to Texas and found a future she'd never imagined. And she'd come to Alabama to get her cowboy back.

Mission accomplished.

"I envision you groveling and maybe cleaning the toilets for a good month," she said, looping her arms about his neck.

He made a face. "Surely you wouldn't make the man you love clean toilets. How about some sexual favors instead?"

"What do you have in mind?" she asked.

"Something where you wear my chaps and I try bucking you off." He grabbed her hips and brought her to him.

"Did you say bucking?"

"Mmm-hmm," he said, dotting her jaw with kisses.

"Okay, deal."

* * * * *

COMING NEXT MONTH FROM

Available February 16, 2016

#883 HER SEXY MARINE VALENTINE
Uniformly Hot!
by Candace Havens
To get past Valentine's Day, new friends Brody Williams and Marigold McGuire are pretending they're in love. But their burning-hot chemistry means the Marine and the interior designer's make-believe is quickly becoming a super-sexy reality...

#884 COMPROMISING POSITIONS
The Wrong Bed
by Kate Hoffmann
One bed. Two owners. Sam Blackstone and Amelia Sheffield are willing to play dirty to get what they want. But at the end of the day, will that be the bed...or each other?

#885 SWEET SEDUCTION
by Daire St. Denis
When Daisy Sinclair finds out the man she spent the night with is her ex-husband's new lawyer, she flips. Is Jamie Forsythe in on helping steal her family bakery? Or was their sweet seduction the real thing?

#886 COWBOY STRONG
Wild Western Heat
by Kelli Ireland
Tyson Covington and Mackenzie Malone were rivals...with benefits. But when Ty is forced to put his future in Kenzie's hands, he has to do something more dangerous than loving the enemy: he has to trust her.

REQUEST YOUR FREE BOOKS!
2 FREE NOVELS PLUS 2 FREE GIFTS!

HARLEQUIN®

Blaze

red-hot reads!

YES! Please send me 2 FREE Harlequin® Blaze® novels and my 2 FREE gifts (gifts are worth about $10). After receiving them, if I don't wish to receive any more books, I can return the shipping statement marked "cancel." If I don't cancel, I will receive 4 brand-new novels every month and be billed just $4.74 per book in the U.S. or $5.21 per book in Canada. That's a savings of at least 14% off the cover price. It's quite a bargain. Shipping and handling is just 50¢ per book in the U.S. and 75¢ per book in Canada.* I understand that accepting the 2 free books and gifts places me under no obligation to buy anything. I can always return a shipment and cancel at any time. Even if I never buy another book, the two free books and gifts are mine to keep forever.

150/350 HDN GH2D

Name	(PLEASE PRINT)

Address	Apt. #

City	State/Prov.	Zip/Postal Code

Signature (if under 18, a parent or guardian must sign)

Mail to the **Reader Service**:
IN U.S.A.: P.O. Box 1867, Buffalo, NY 14240-1867
IN CANADA: P.O. Box 609, Fort Erie, Ontario L2A 5X3

Want to try two free books from another line?
Call 1-800-873-8635 or visit www.ReaderService.com.

* Terms and prices subject to change without notice. Prices do not include applicable taxes. Sales tax applicable in N.Y. Canadian residents will be charged applicable taxes. Offer not valid in Quebec. This offer is limited to one order per household. Not valid for current subscribers to Harlequin Blaze books. All orders subject to credit approval. Credit or debit balances in a customer's account(s) may be offset by any other outstanding balance owed by or to the customer. Please allow 4 to 6 weeks for delivery. Offer available while quantities last.

Your Privacy—The Reader Service is committed to protecting your privacy. Our Privacy Policy is available online at www.ReaderService.com or upon request from the Reader Service.

We make a portion of our mailing list available to reputable third parties that offer products we believe may interest you. If you prefer that we not exchange your name with third parties, or if you wish to clarify or modify your communication preferences, please visit us at www.ReaderService.com/consumerchoice or write to us at Reader Service Preference Service, P.O. Box 9062, Buffalo, NY 14240-9062. Include your complete name and address.

HB15

*Daisy Sinclair is determined to get over the
embarrassment of Colin Forsythe accidentally
seeing her naked…something that he didn't seem
to mind at all!*

Read on for a sneak preview of
SWEET SEDUCTION
by New York Times *bestselling author*
Daire St. Denis

"Ms. Sinclair?"

Daisy looked up at the man standing in the doorway to her office. Yes, he was Colin Forsythe all right. His wavy brown hair might have been a bit longer than in the picture beside his column, but he had the same square jaw, the same nose—though in person it was a little crooked—and the same full lips. While he was recognizable, his byline picture did not do him justice. In that picture he came off as stern, albeit in a well-coiffed, intellectual sort of way. In person? Wow. He looked anything but. His eyes sparkled with irreverence, his lips turned up at one side as if he was trying to keep a sinful smile in check, and he was just…bigger. More like a professional athlete than a distinguished foodie.

His eyebrows rose under her appraisal. "Do I pass?"

Daisy cringed. Good-looking. Big ego. No surprise. Obviously, he was going to make this impossible for her. But he was Colin Forsythe, and she'd been anticipating this interview ever since taking over Nana Sin's bakery three years ago. Of course he had to show up today of all days.

"Can we pretend, for my sake, that we're meeting for the first time, right now? That you didn't just…" Daisy paused to take a deep, composing breath. "Hello, Mr. Forsythe." She walked around her desk, hand outstretched. "I'm Daisy Sinclair. Welcome to Nana Sin's."

He rubbed his jaw as if trying to massage his face into a serious expression. It didn't work. When she was close enough, he took her hand and shook it firmly. "It's Colin."

"Colin." She set her lips in a grim line and sauntered past, head held high. At the door she turned. "Shall we?"

"Shall we what?"

Daisy rolled her eyes. "Aren't you here to see the bakery?"

In one step Colin was beside her, looking down at her. Damn, the man was tall. Not fair. And what the hell was he doing, blasting her with that sinful smile of his?

"I've already seen everything." He grinned.

She groaned.

He came closer, spoke more softly. "What I'd really like is a taste."

The way he looked at her made Daisy think he wanted to taste her.

Don't miss
SWEET SEDUCTION
by Daire St. Denis,
available March 2016 wherever
Harlequin® Blaze® books and ebooks are sold.

www.Harlequin.com

Turn your love of reading into rewards you'll love with

Harlequin My Rewards

**Join for FREE today at
www.HarlequinMyRewards.com**

Earn **FREE BOOKS** of your choice.

Experience **EXCLUSIVE OFFERS** and contests.

Enjoy **BOOK RECOMMENDATIONS**
selected just for you.

PLUS! Sign up now
and get **500** points
right away!

Earn
FREE
REWARDS
Join
Today!
HarlequinMyRewards.com

MYR16R

Looking for more wealthy bachelors? Fear not!
Be sure to collect these sexy reads from
Harlequin® Presents and Harlequin® Desire!

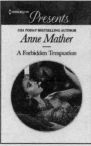

A FORBIDDEN TEMPTATION
by Anne Mather

Jack Connolly isn't looking for a woman—
until he meets Grace Spencer! Trapped in a
fake relationship to safeguard her family,
Grace knows giving in to Jack would risk
everything she holds dear… But will she
surrender to the forbidden?

Available February 16, 2016

SNOWBOUND WITH THE BOSS
(Pregnant by the Boss)
by Maureen Child

When gaming tycoon Sean Ryan is
stranded with irascible, irresistible contractor
Kate Wells, the temptation to keep each other
warm proves overwhelming. Dealing with
unexpected feelings is hard enough, but what
about an unexpected pregnancy? They're
about to find out…

Available March 1, 2016

THE WORLD IS BETTER WITH

Romance

Harlequin has everything from contemporary, passionate and heartwarming to suspenseful and inspirational stories.

Whatever your mood, we have a romance just for you!

SERIESHALOAD2015